My Child is a Stranger:

Stories

by

B. W. Teigland

AOS Publishing, 2024
Copyright © 2024

B. W. Teigland

ISBN: 978-1-990496-89-9

Cover Design: Jessica James

Visit AOS Publishing's website:
www.aospublishing.com

Contents

My Child is a Stranger

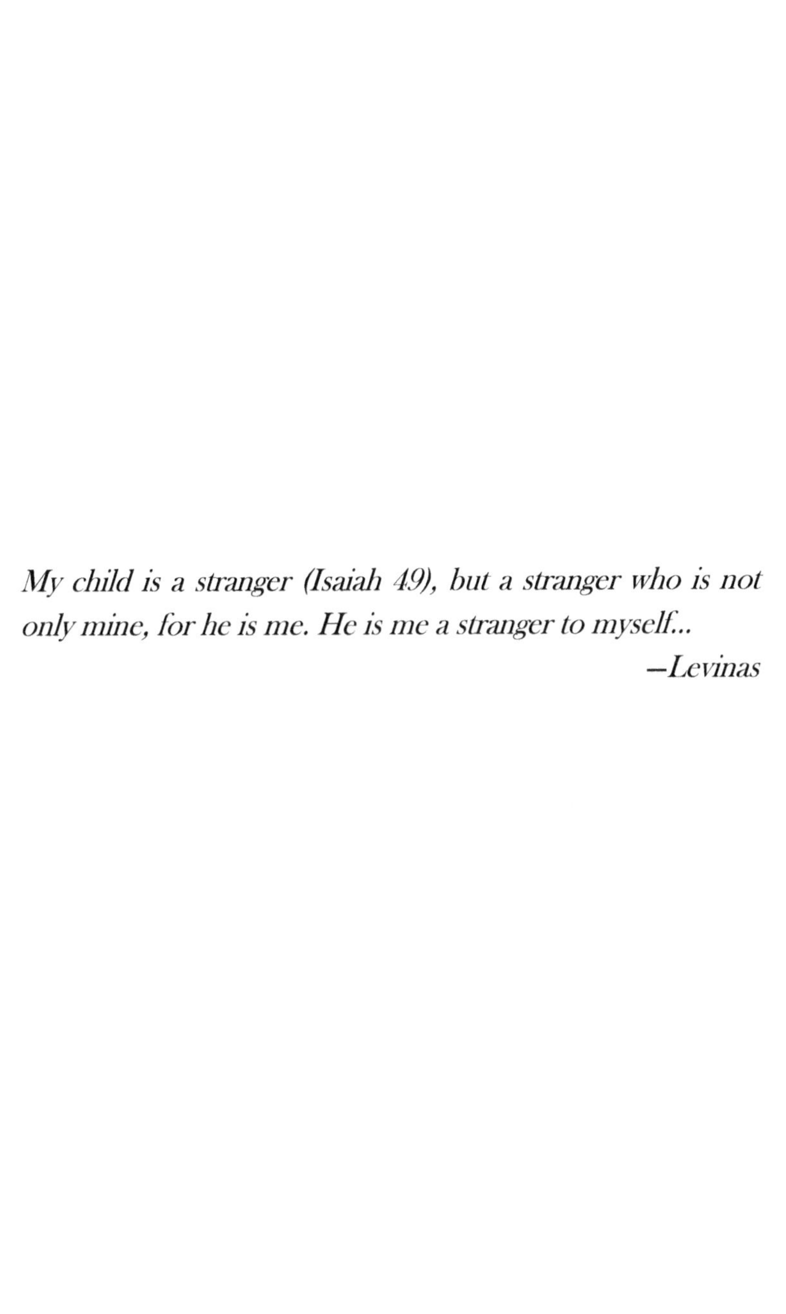

My child is a stranger (Isaiah 49), but a stranger who is not only mine, for he is me. He is me a stranger to myself...
—Levinas

Ad Nauseam

Out of the water, the walrus has bad eyesight. When it drags its thousand-pound body out of the ocean, out and up, it can no longer see where it is. But it has found a place to rest, away from its pod. It has climbed the sea cliff.

The spot where the walrus would have rested—the spot where nature deemed it should rest, the spot where the salty foam of the sea meets the shore, a thousand feet below—this spot has become so overcrowded with rival walruses that it has become safer to take this evolutionary drunken walk away from its part and share in that animal kingdom.

In the entire history of walruses, the animal has not done this before. Not until now, at the North Pole, where the polar caps are melting earlier each year, leaving the walrus high and dry, broken by weariness, vertically pushed outside the pod.

Uneasy, the walrus falls asleep on the open cliff and spends the night alone, not with the herd of walruses. Then the walrus wakes up on the edge of the precipice. Sensing that the rest of its pod is below, it tries to go back the only way it can—the way it came. Down the cliff.

Using flippers and not wings, it slides on the loose rock, somersaults, falls the one thousand feet, and is crushed, blubber and bone, by its impact with the rocky seashore. It jerks convulsively and dies.

Not just one walrus. Herds of walrus share the same fate, the same fatal destiny.

The polar bear hunts seals. But the sea ice is melting in the Arctic. So it cannot hunt seals, cannot stand motionless for hours at the seals' breathing holes. Unable, just like the walrus, to solve the problem of failing life, the maritime bear swims to the shore below the cliff from which the walruses have been jumping.

The polar bear usually eats enough to see it through eight long months of eating absolutely nothing. But having eaten only one seal, only eight days' worth of energy, the polar bear is hungry again and so will swim the distance to the northern cape, to the cove of suicidal walruses. And in doing so it will risk drowning or being killed by orcas, which eat the seals that the polar bear did not, which will happen more and more in the years to come, when the ice has melted completely: from solid to liquid, from glacial silence to nothing yet known.

Not just one polar bear. Many will make this trip.

The cubs quickly learn the new ritual from their parents. After striking the hollow carcasses in playful imitation of the hunt, they eat the walruses.

At one time, polar bears and walruses were equal predators—equal in strength, in body mass, in aggression and instinct. But not now. Not now that the walruses are hurling themselves against the steep, jagged rocks.

In turn, seabirds dive. They glide into the watery mass, into the old ocean, and swim, forcing back the aquatic layers with the bones of their wings. Whales roar, and their huge mouths filter krill through baleen systems—krill that feeds on the polar lichen growing below the edge of an iceberg. Ice floes crash incessantly against each other when the ice breaks up in the polar sea. And under all the power of the narwhal's spiral tusks, which migrate through fissures in the sea ice, millions of diatoms are spontaneously born.

The obstacle of survival is everywhere, so much so that it is not untrue to say that life is an obstacle. And that obstacle, varying as it does in the trials it offers, is indifferent. All things on the planet are connected through this indifference. And all things become one thing.

The Last Shape

I have a frightful recurring dream.

I'm in the Ancient Bristlecone Pine Forest in Inyo County, curled into the fetal position. Above me are twisted, gnarled trunks. Their branches are mostly stripped of foliage. And I am stripped of all my worldly belongings. There I seem to stay, forever, among all the other humans who hope to return to the womb of the earth. We've forgotten where the entrance is, and so we remain in the purgatory of that vast, listening forest.

These human beings came to plant themselves here and grow. And grow they do—up and down and side to side, spiraling to the outermost bounds of the night. But the shape they hope for is not the shape they take.

At this special place in the White Mountains of California, the bristlecone pines twist with the planet's rotation. They wrap five thousand years of secrets into the blond highlights of their bark—secrets that must be kept by Methuselah in a grove of the wickedest desires to leave humanity.

There, in this frightful recurring dream, I have a frightful recurring thought: longevity leads to lunacy.

I'm on an expedition into the White Mountains. The rangers give the public the impression that they know, but aren't at liberty to say, where the Methuselah is. "To prevent vandals from desecrating it," they say on the sly. But if you read the journals that document the original discovery, as I have, you'll get another impression altogether.

The dendrochronologist Edmund Schulman didn't claim to have found the actual Methuselah. Rather, he claimed that this forest in the White Mountains was the keeper of a species of tree that exceeded the age of any other living organism. He blatantly told scholars he didn't know the oldest tree's exact coordinates.

It's still out there, agelessly outliving the world. If he had found it, we wouldn't know its name or his. Together, they would have remained an unknown unknown.

After a day's searching, I arrive at the summit of an unnamed mountain and set up camp. Then I reach for the rations in my rucksack—vacuum-sealed meals that I prepared and portioned several days back. They taste as good as fresh.

I gaze down. The windward side of the mountain is taking on the night. From this vantage, straddling the peak, I'm as present as the enormous shadow that seems to come out from the stone. It spreads like a flood, establishing a current, until one side is dark. Then the shadow drenches the mountain peak. I surrender to it.

With nothing to burn, I let my eyes adjust to the dark. Over the next thirty minutes, the rod cells in my retinas open like nocturnal flowers, and, in turn, the cone cells close. It's as if my vision blossoms from an arbour rather than an eye.

My lungs catch the cool air like the wings of a peppered moth as it flies over an industrial boneyard. To stop breathing would be as easy as ripping the wings off this same moth.

Growing eerie in the spectral pallor of moonlight, the wispy trees—squat, spiraling, and conical—ache to touch the threatening sky. Their seeds scatter, adapt, resist, and survive. Ecological hackers of a terrain full of limitations. The knots in the wood are hard and tight. They are dead and still, but alive with something I don't yet know how to articulate.

I sit alone in that pale moonlight, and it's as if I'm being led into sleep through another passage. My recurring dream is happening all on its own, with no need for a sleeper.

Methuselah reveals secrets to those who seek truth and fail. The path to it is divided, each forked line marked by a numinous event in the *mysterium tremendum*. A mystery before which humanity both trembles and is fascinated, by which we are both repelled and attracted.

At the forked path is a metaphorical figure. It's the shadow of five thousand trees shifting their place, the motion of something not quite there but with enough detail to cause doubt. It's the shadow of the unearthly casting itself against a panorama of night sky—the last shape of nevermore and its featureless plain of silence, morphing into the evermore.

I scan my notes during the next day's rest stops. Famous aestheticians have written lengthy commentaries contesting Methuselah's last shape, which I've saved on my phone:

"It is everything and nothing at once—the very shape of shapelessness itself!"
—*NATURELESS ECOLOGY*

"Following the golden ratio, the final shape would be a divine shape, a platonic ideal."
—*A TIME FOR ERROR*

"A flame of motion, a burning bush that is never consumed by life, though figuratively burns with another death. For flame and speech are original accomplices—the bush in the desert does not burn for itself alone, but always for itself and the prophet."
—*VAN DIJK*

Of course, this is all folk wisdom and salacious lore. I have had the dream so many times—probably a result of the ominous myths that have sat in my head at night, like undigested food sits in one's stomach. In the tedium of those sleepless hours, I've been able to narrow down the forking path it takes me on over satellite images of the area, like a GPS map service, though I'm not sure if the directions even matter. I follow it as if carried along by a fever dream.

I was officially on tour. The first conference was held in Los Angeles. An expert panelist was needed to help substantiate the topic of humanity's pursuit of immortality, but the organizers couldn't have anticipated what I would find. Just before we went on camera, the television journalist, her face haggard around desperate eyes, explained to the audience that they would only edit for time. What she really meant was that a computer program would censor parts of my response in every time zone but the one we were in.

"Professor Abbasi, those you have accused of holding 'ecologically conservative ideologies' have recently described you as a provocateur. Your newest publication, *Can One Be Content with One Hundred Years of Awareness?*, was controversially received by your critics. In it, you deny the existence of nature, because you believe that nature has, quote, 'Become a higher authority, comparable to religion.'

"Truth be told, you inveigle people into theophany. You ensnare them, in so many words, to believe that a visible manifestation of nature is equivalent to a god in construct, and then you say it is the power of this construct we must concern ourselves with. Why would you think environmental catastrophes are being politically staged, and what do you mean when you claim that nature should be re-understood as completely artificial abstract materialism?"

"~~You think~~ I'm an environmental terrorist because I want to see your garbage in nature reserves ~~and not being covertly used to contaminate at-risk communities through the politics of space, fine, but~~ don't act surprised when you don't understand ~~a landfill~~," I said. "Waste is progress. ~~The sooner~~ this planet is a slumland, ~~the sooner you'll see that building a new one was the only option you had left.~~"

Her forehead wrinkled as she studied me. Her eyes, as hard as green pebbles, were clouded with perplexity. "Nature and the planet are usually seen as one and the same. How can you possibly separate them? Aren't you committing animism of some kind?"

"Every planet begins and ends ~~lifeless and natureless,~~" I replied. "For a planet to be uninhabited is highly probable. ~~Planets are the skeletons of space, the bones of nothing, from which nature may or may not spawn.~~ Nature cannot take us ~~any~~ farther. ~~Not because~~ we ~~don't~~ believe in it ~~enough, but because the planet, insofar as it may be anthropomorphized to illustrate my point, has stopped believing in nature. The planet itself is a nihilist.~~ The planet has ~~lost~~ faith in us."

She was in an awkward position now, tasked with deciding what was and what wasn't important about my candour. "You have decided to speak very little about the discoveries made in your longevity studies, and much about the fate of the world. What brought on this change of perspective? Some would say it's not your place to judge outside your discipline."

"Oh, horse feathers. It's precisely my place to socialize my and my colleagues' findings. With longer life comes more awareness, and how much more awareness is enough to make it right? Death, the major environmental constraint, has been lifted. My book was meant to shed light on ~~the moral obligation taken on by~~ those who live beyond one hundred years of awareness, ~~which I have not personally seen upheld.~~ Nature is not designed for immortals. As it is, it lives ~~off mortality.~~ But in evaluating some of my patients who have been successfully immortalized, I see that they are a ~~de~~humanization of other sentient beings. They become ~~in~~different. They become planets without nature."

I said this, or something like it, again and again as the tour dates continued. They just wanted me to tell them I knew the cure for death. That I knew the secret for life everlasting. They didn't want to know what that meant for everyone else.

They didn't want to know about environmental racism. About the people who can only afford to live where garbage burns, about the stink in the air that's now in the fibres of their clothing as well. In them grow rare forms of cancer.

They didn't want the hypocrisy of their pathological immigration ideologies to be known. A mother could drop the hand of one of her children to save the other, could drown in the Mediterranean herself and gain sympathy, but the child who was given room on the raft, turned into a refugee, and failed by the state wouldn't receive that understanding.

Scientists are accountable for the full implications of their research. You can make a lot of mistakes in just one lifetime. But that's not what my fiscal sponsors thought. I was a saint to some and a devil to others, and that's how it would stay.

The tour is days behind me now, and I walk ahead, along these borders of silence. Even through the cover of a great and ancient forest, there still grows upon my ears the distant sound of the vehement populous. The big media machine with its brutal and careless strength. Regathering views on my tell-all. Failing to perceive any limitations in the symbols in which the media traps us. Black spots dance before their eyes as information consumes attention and attention alone, as brains merge with a controlled digital space. And after years of interviews, I find no solace in the fact that this place is the only place where nothing makes sense. My belief that I have experienced things that never happened and the sketches that fill my dream journal are evidence of these un-verdant mountains holding more than they hold, being more than they are.

According to Genesis 5:27, Methuselah was the oldest human to have ever lived. Unlike his father, Enoch, who didn't die but was taken by God, he died as all humans do, but only after nine hundred and sixty-nine years on earth.

Whether the age was a mistranslation or a myth, it doesn't matter much, because either way, his death marked the year of the flood and the end of the ten-generational sequence from Adam to Noah. Time enough for the world to be destroyed by human desire.

For Schulman to have found the Methuselah, he would have had to have this in mind. I myself think it's pseudo-thought, but I can appreciate the comparison between a religious anomaly and a scientific one: a point in time at which no human being will experience death.

For humans, it was the curse of Mitochondrial Eve that brought on the aging process. The earth's oxidation rusted the carbon ocean and created a living and dying atmosphere. The free radical of a normal metabolism is a by-product whose accumulation results in a similar damage in humans. Eve was the radical of Adam. A normal immortality was the driving force of mortality. On a biological level, Mitochondrial Eve brought the aging process to Adam through the genetics of her species.

Proper waste management became necessary. There evolved a collection of techniques that would rejuvenate the damage caused by the human body's essential metabolic processes, on both a molecular and cellular level, postponing age-associated diseases. My biogerontology is admittedly speculative, though that doesn't make it any less scientific. The span of one thousand years is assuredly within our lifetime.

Lobsters and hydras are among some of the only species to show no symptoms of aging. They predate trees. Their bodies engineer longevity. But the bristlecone pines are another matter altogether—in most of those with extreme lifespans, only the roots are still alive at the latest stage, and everything above the alkaline surface is simply deadwood. They grow in the place where no competition is possible. We humans, too, will have to go to such extreme environmental points to reach beyond survival.

You have to be half dead to be half alive.

Staring up at the dark mass of trees above the dim shadow of the slopes, I look at myself again as I looked at myself the day before I came to the mountain. In my head are the thoughts I may have had, and the thoughts I maybe didn't have—the thoughts that had been part of the dream.

Now I have an opportunity to prove the mettle of my dreamquest, and yet that first conference still weighs on my mind. I decide to use some of my phone's battery life to pull up my essay from the conference. Recordings of it were probably already circling the world through social media before I even left the state. I imagine there will be an unanswerable number of emails when I return, though I'm sure my assistant can easily impersonate me for now.

I read through some of my more controversial paragraphs, the ones that I'll have to defend with a new book in the coming years, to avoid being marked a sensationalist and possibly lynched by critics. I imagine that the panelists—experts on sustainability, conservation geology, climate modeling, and environmental history—were both scared and thrilled as they shot me vengeful stares. I swipe across the screen:

"To immortalize themselves, some creatures have habit, others have science. The first indication that a species is preparing for immortalization is the mechanism of serialization. They arrange their futures in a series of repeating and predictable events. Our serialization, on an individual basis and as a culture, will be what we will attempt to translate from data structures or object states into a format that can be stored, transmitted, and reconstructed later.

"The next stage, one that we are arguably already in, the serialization having already taken place, is taking the jump itself. Or, as the overused Kuhnian expression goes, the paradigm shift. This jump or shift, as we have seen in the extinction of so many species, is one of eliminative selection.

"And this is where my theory has changed. Until now, I naively spent my energies on the internal mechanisms of agelessness, when it was the environment that I should have naturally taken into consideration. It takes everything to be a god, all the resources and more still, similar to the metabolism of capitalism. Capitalism recognized that only a few can sustain the immortal state once the mechanisms are in place and did away with the remainder, people who didn't bring in profit. Immortality is an industry of doubt—a dangerous product that shouldn't be on the market.

"We are in an epoch where those who reach the Methuselarity will need to exploit those pre-moderns who haven't reached it. And those pre-moderns will have to be fully compliant to be exploited. I say this not because of my research but because of the PR strategists I refuse to stand beside.

"For it takes a whole cosmology to sustain just one god, let alone billions."

I miss my return flight and head east. As my feet move, I'm not sure what's taking me further—my scientific inquiries or the pressing nature of my dreams. What can I possibly prove to myself that I don't already know from my research? Whatever it is, I somehow know it will be found in the mirages of these dusty white mountains.

It seems like there is one Ali who attends conferences, who is established as a community member in the culture of science, and another Ali inside the first who needs to be part of that second culture, the one science has nothing to do with. And now this second one, the one who would be recognized by any of the panelists back at the conference, stands on a mountain at the edge of the forest.

Barren and without needles, the most ancient of the trees were naught but saplings during the building of the pyramids. The way to Methuselah is guided by the cones they no longer drop.

The bristlecone pines are everywhere. Nothing dares challenge the sandy territory they sink into. No other organism senses the value of this mountain range like they do. The gods have their privacy at this altitude. The specific conditions allow them to thrive where many others would die. The dirt is white and dry and lacking in nutrients. Desert flowers bloom placenta-purple, and the brows of receding snowdrifts melt each day only to reform from the condensation of the mornings that follow. The trees of this forest have the trance of fire about them, carved, as they are, by the elemental gods that surround the haunting landscape.

As I close in on the mountain's apex, I can make out a graveyard of wood figures.

Here the dream that wasn't a dream becomes that sticky internal contradiction between fact and feeling. I could have taken medication to kill the dream and said the PR pitch like the corporations wanted. Or I could never have investigated biogerontology. Or I could never have become a scientist. Or I could never have been born. But I am here and I am in a reality that points dreamward instead of homeward. I feel I am past the point of choice.

On arrival I see them, and I can only imagine what they see when they see me. Unlike a cross, these wood figures do not speak. Like a cross, the wood figures inspire fear and trembling, being and nothingness, ardency and hysteria. The lost shapes of nevermore jut out of the earth in an ugly manner, like the joints of a frightening limb. A deadwood forest of bristlecone. A boneyard of ancient things. The living aspect of those trees is in the heartwood of their roots, and whatever is in their roots is now moving through the rest of the unspeaking wood skeletons, as if through a cycle of transpiration, filling the surrounding air with a luminous mist. The gaseous entity scales the windward side of the mountain with absolute silence. In the mist, the forest loses its shape, becomes shapeless except for that last shape, which is utterly amorphous in a way that defines it.

Whatever it *actually* is seems to animate the forest roots with a living breath—the *nefesh*, or moving air, the *ruach*, or spirit wind, feeling, passion, thought.

The oldest, the Methuselah, is not any tree in particular but rather the entire spirit of the forest. The nameless mist is not only a thing—it's a place. Like a flock of starlings, it moves in murmurations over the bonelike whiteness of the mountaintops.

What the forest exhales is outside of time and space. I realize in the throes of this revelation that these trees live an unnaturally long existence because what's in their roots is *not of this existence.* They coexist as though a whole bacterial galaxy is hidden away inside them.

Falling prey to this revelation, I exclaim, and it listens: "The blown breath—breath of the gods!"

Had this species outlasted all others in holding in the divine breath of life? Methuselah is nothing if not the last Adamic vessel, manifesting the breath that life took before it was expelled from the earth's lung. And then it occurs to me that the Biblical flood was the doom of drowning in water, but *our* flood is a sea of airlessness.

The secret message: at the heart of their roots, the miraculous trees store the breath of life. The roots breathe with the world in mutual animation and subjectivity. These breath-entities must have been an ancient technology of the gods. They breathed on everything and in return the breathers breathed back, the necessary twin in a primary dual.

My journey up the mountain was one of silence. It is more than silent now. The air is gone, my breath sucked out of me, and now another ethereal being is transpiring where it has been removed. Through some kind of occult breath science, I can not breathe. But I am not dead.

The *nefesh* remains for a moment, lingering as a cloud would in the saturnine sky. It dissipates and becomes thinner than air. On last inspection, the trees are all dead to their roots. They sink like snakes into the thirsty ground.

After my sojourn on the White Mountains, I went home. It was finally time to go home, but home was not the same. To this day, my breath has not returned to me. The canal is gone, the lungs are closed, and I pretend to breathe.

People breathe as they always have. The air has changed, but they have not. And with each breath they take they can't help but make the customary motions of that long-forgotten prayer—a superstitious habit, showing their devotion to the cathedral of the planet, to an atmosphere composed of atheism and asthma, catharsis and carbon.

But a new god breathes through me now. And whatever breathes in us is us.

City 40

Resignation to one's fate takes practice. Or so citizen Yauza maintained. He began every day with an exercise. It went like this: he walked to a wall, put his back up against it, and stood there in infinite resignation. After a minute or two, it was over. He could begin to live.

The people of City 40 lived inside "the box." The box was a secret and they lived inside it. Outside the box, there were places that had names. But inside the box, the people remained nameless. And like Schrödinger's cat, while the citizens of the nameless town were inside the box, it was unknown whether they were dead or alive. Probably, they were simultaneously dead and alive.

The town that might or might not have been a town had no name. It was simply called Chelyabinsk-40. Chelyabinsk was the closest city in the oblast, so people like Yauza—who knew of the existence of the town and so had reason to talk about it, working for the Russian Post as he did—used the last digits of its one and only postal-box number to identify it.

Chelyabinsk-40 had no post office, so Yauza had to drive his mobile post van, a van that bore the Byzantine double-headed eagle emblem in the flag's tsarist tricolours, from Chelyabinsk to Chelyabinsk-40, providing all the services that would have been available had it had a post office of its own.

Yauza's deliveries were always delayed. He insisted that it was not out of ineffectiveness but because the Russian Post just had too many official functions to overcome the pressure of the many social factors involved. Postmats, automated machines, had just been deployed in the southern Urals. All he had to do in Chelyabinsk-40 was make the now-automatic issue of shipments available. In other words, he only had to load the postmat with new mail, which came from one of the major automated regional sorting centres.

He sometimes felt that even he himself, Yauza, citizen Yauza, like the postmat and the major automated regional sorting centres, was an automaton.

The postmat was located inside the facility's ice-covered gates, fenced in by barbed wire on all sides and heavily monitored. He was escorted by armed guards to and from this community postmat, and often never said a word to them. The chevron-shaped furrows on the guards' brow squinted through ordinary people, such as Yauza, as through glass. The facility at Chelyabinsk-40 didn't resemble a plant used for heavy industry but rather a bureau of design and scientific research. A place where design and matter met.

The Mayak plant and those in that residential district, the most infamous of all closed cities, perhaps the biggest box (though who really knew enough to compare), was close to here. The plant still processed nuclear waste and recycled nuclear material from decommissioned nuclear weapons of the Cold War years.

Chelyabinsk-40 was a remote place, deep in the Urals and Siberian backwaters. He didn't like knowing about it. Mostly because it wasn't good to know too much about anything secret. The rumours had always been that people living in closed cities lived better than the rest. From what Yauza had seen, this didn't seem to be true.

The days that he went to the box were, according to Yauza, the days that didn't exist. Days of his life were circumscribed by barbed wire, oppressed by implied captivity because of secrets that were not his own. The suffocating soullessness of those streets and the terrestrial magnificence that lay just outside the limits of the closed town.

Today, at the end of the drive, after an agonizing two-hour drive to the box and then back again from it, Yauza decided to stop for an hour or so outside the city of Chelyabinsk, at Lake Chebarkul, to smoke and stretch his stiff limbs.

The Ural Mountains glowed greenish-violet in the last daylight and began to turn red-violet in the incandescent light of the night sky. Against the dark sky before sunset, noctilucent clouds glowed electric blue. Crystalline ice seeded the clouds in the high-altitude light. A huge nimbus surrounded by darkness. A mysterious light source. A noctilucent cloud at the edge of space.

Formed along the shore of the lake was the town of Chebarkul, considerably less closed off from the world than Chelyabinsk-40 but still as much a poor Siberian town as any he'd seen. Not far from where he was standing, ground into the sand around the lake, was a rain-rusted cartridge clip from a rifle and a few miserable fossilized Soviet rubles he'd found buried in a tin. Earlier in his commute, Yauza had seen a tank in similar condition, under a bridge, flipped onto its back like a turtle that's been in brumation for over half a century. Both were from the days when Russians talked among themselves with gunshots.

With wind-chapped lips, Yauza smoked a rolled-tobacco cigarette through his beard, which was the colour of fog. The wind batted about his earflaps, which were turned down under a particoloured fur hat. From where he stood, the black cavities of windows stretching across the shoreline resembled eye sockets. He could just barely see a red-lit window in a dilapidated church, abandoned in a field on the other side of the road, opposite the town.

On its roof was a single dome that resembled an onion, the bulbous structure tapering smoothly to a point. From afar it looked more like a burning candle. No snow gathered on this roof, and Yauza thought maybe this was why the structure had been built this way. The natural wood was showing under the colourful paint, and under the overhang, it was missing several walls. He couldn't help but think of that ancient three-letter word: G-o-d. God. The ultimate noun.

The light went off and on, and off and on, much like a broken lighter. Laughing like a match. "Vagabonds or anarchists or... evil spirits, I guess? Ghouls, maybe?" He spat out a flake of tobacco and decided he would ask around about it after getting a drink at the town's bar.

The vodka was good and he felt warm and sure. Yauza took saccharin in the next, throwing back its contents and swallowing it all in one manly gulp before angrily slamming his glass on the bar. The drive to the box always put him in a bitter state. Now that the alcohol had warmed him to the bone, his puffy face was red, and even his nose seemed swollen. His eyes were drawn to the tiny, momentary pearls in his glass and, like a drunk, he stared into his next vodka before drinking it.

Yauza took off his greasy fur hat, folded it, and put it in the pocket of his thick jacket, revealing the round bald spot that resembled an eye at the back of his head.

Through the light-blue smoke, the mahogany bar shone like gold. The porter rattled the miscellaneous metal cans of his meandering trade as if they were a bunch of absurd hollow keys. The corpses of glasses and bottles, their lights exploding, rang like a battery of little bells when the bartender touched them together. The peals emanating from the bottles reminded him that he wanted to ask about the flickering red light in the church's dark window.

The light was as brief as the burning of a match, though an entire matchbox must have been wasted by the effort, Yauza thought, behind his eyes. *But what if this red light was a proliferating hallucination that only I can see? A hallucination that intensified, causing the pseudo-occurrence to multiply into a pseudo-world. The relation between external reality and human consciousness is a strange one. For everything you see has a special meaning to you chiefly because you see it. To me because I see it.*

He decided he needed to prove his nerves false.

"Another bottle!" somebody said to the bartender. "Turn the fire up, too. There's a terrible draft." The door was wedged open; it wouldn't close properly.

Yauza gathered himself together but didn't immediately rush over to these miserable people at this miserable time of night, alone and sleepless, waiting together for dawn.

In the cracked light shining weakly around the green baize of the billiard table, eight drowsy figures stood with their elbows propped up on its sides, pulling out fistfuls of money from their pockets and dropping them in undignified ways, swallowing great glugs of beer all the while.

Yauza approached the large, drunken circle, the oily floor sticking to the soles of his heavy, well-worn boots. The figures fiercely scrutinized the newcomer, trying quickly to guess what had brought him here, why his glass was trembling in his hand, and what he had to hide.

Yauza retrieved some paper money and coins from his own jacket's pocket and, as he was doing so, accidentally collided with one of the men holding a glass of beer. The glass tipped over and left a pool of beer on the baize cloth. The pool described the shape of a flattened, uncertain animal before soaking into the table completely.

When Yauza turned to beg the man's pardon, he received an unexpected punch in the mouth.

Yauza woke up at a table in the back room playing with two loose molars in his upper jaw. He ran the tip of his tongue over his swollen lips and felt a thick, congealed lump that tasted both bitter and sweet. There was a deep gash in his cheek. Someone had given him a proper socking in the face. His money was gone. The back of his head was sore, and there was an enormous welt smarting where there hadn't been one smarting before. *Probably from falling back onto that oily floor,* Yauza thought blurrily, from under a puzzled brow.

He found the bar empty, abandoned, the people in it invisibilized by time, and a note stuck to the door stating, in capital letters, "GET OUT." Yauza left through the permanently wedged-open door.

It was snowing. The air was a cindery grey. It was just before dawn. The post-midnight footprints, sunken down into the drifts, were already covered by flatteringly soft snow. He decided to walk straight across the frozen lake, as he'd done before to get to the decrepit hole of a bar.

A burning odour blackened the air, leaden like gunpowder, and a needle-like chill threaded its way through Yauza's body. His eyelids quivered and his head filled with a dark emotion.

There came three incandescent lights. Three stars that seemed to mock Yauza as they rose like huge torching columns on the horizon. Above them were three suns. *Sun dogs, maybe, or it could be from the blow I took to the head.* A second later, these three lights became one and shook the sky, and then the frozen lake he was still walking on also shook. The scorching intensity of the sudden object hurtling toward him battered his senses, sending Yauza sprawling and diving face-first into the cold snow.

He screamed as sparks sprayed around him and the core of the light hit, colliding with the ground somewhere in front of him. His teeth smashed in his mouth, his bones turned to powder. The reverberation lived within him as he tried to regain his footing, even as the impact conjured up an enormous tidal wave. When it fell upon him, the weight, the immensity, destroyed him once more and washed away anything he could have recognized, could have known. He gasped and thrashed and hurt.

The tidal wave faded. The burning lights receded.

Uppgivenhetssyndrom

Dr. Evelyn Volk wasn't happy. Nor did she feel as though she deserved much happiness. No one like her did. More and more she felt as if she were pressing her head deeper and deeper into the earth, looking for the ostrich's sand-buried dreams. And after just one look at the children with *Uppgivenhetssyndrom* she knew, irrefutably, that she'd have to provide these refugee families with consultations free of charge.

"Do what you can within the limits of your abilities" was all the advice she'd received from other Swedish doctors, even though she'd treated over forty children with resignation syndrome. In the last two years alone there had been more reported cases than all the other reported cases combined since the syndrome was first identified. "Because most of us still don't know if what we're dealing with here is just medicine or simply politics. Exhausting, complicated, intricate politics."

The Swedish doctors didn't know for certain whether this disorder, this dissociative syndrome that mainly affected young people, was a culture-bound one among children of asylum seekers from former Soviet and Yugoslavian countries, refugees from the Balkans, Yazidis from Iraq, and children from the persecuted Roma minority. Perhaps it was just some mysterious illness. Regardless, the Swedish doctors weren't sure that the asylum-seeking parents weren't abusing their own children while the families waited for the resolution of their asylum claims in Sweden.

So Dr. Evelyn Volk went to medical professionals outside Sweden. They'd never heard of such a thing happening anywhere else. There was, as of yet, no known case identified. Not since World War II, in the concentration camps.

She also visited several towns within Sweden. In these places, the refugee children's story was passed on as if it were a fairy tale—

a fairy tale about how children just stopped walking, stopped talking, and stopped eating. And then these same children, with this so-called resignation syndrome, assumed a coma-like state, lying prone with their eyes closed, disconnected. In response to which Dr. Evelyn Volk followed the advice of the other Swedish doctors and did what she could within the limits of her abilities. She showed the parents how to feed these children via feeding tubes and explained the potential complications of these feeding tubes.

Meanwhile, the Swedish Migration Board's fear of refugees overburdening the welfare system and public resources only deepened, making the otherwise "refugee-friendly" Swedes increasingly concerned about the country's refugees per capita in relation to the rest of Europe. Regardless of how much their refusal to take in more refugees had contributed to the increase in known cases of the syndrome over the last two years, the board still rejected the hundred thousand people who applied for asylum in Sweden. These families who just showed up, again and again, from all sorts of places, were told that they wouldn't be able to stay in the country—absolutely no asylum, no three-year residency permit, no new claims, and definitely no underground living.

As Dr. Evelyn Volk saw it, the Swedish Migration Board only had to raise the barricade that they themselves had built. "Since, as Swedish doctors very well know," Dr. Evelyn Volk said to the Swedish Migration Board, "these cases are dependent on a sense of security and the positive resolution of their families' asylum claims here in Sweden."

*

First, Aleksander was extorted. Then, they violently beat him and his wife. Their nine-year-old daughter, Sofya, witnessed all the bloody blows laid upon her parents. Finally, the Mafia kidnapped him. But he survived.

Having survived the extortion, the violent beatings, and even the kidnapping, he fled Russia with his family. No sooner had Aleksander and his wife and daughter arrived in Frankfurt than they were overstaying their tourist visas. Eventually they took a train to Sweden, where they lived underground until they could no longer be sent back to Germany under the Dublin Regulation.

It wasn't easy for the Swedes to send Aleksander and his family back to Russia once they emerged from hiding and filed an application for asylum.

Aleksander and his family were terrified of the Mafia, who had extorted, beaten, and kidnapped Aleksander. In Russia, it was considered treason to apply for asylum, but that's what Aleksander did. He became a traitor, after which he and his family received a three-year residency permit in Sweden. Aleksander was eventually able to find work in construction, even though he'd once been in the tech industry, and so he was a construction worker for three long years.

In Russia, Aleksander had been involved in what could be called a samizdat Internet service: the service of copying and distributing information banned by the Communist state; that is to say, reproducing censored and underground publications via the Internet.

When Aleksander's temporary residency permit expired, he could only apply for the permanent residency permit. And he and his family were rejected.

The Swedish Migration Board sent word of the decision via a letter. One day later, the board sent a confirmation letter to ensure that Aleksander and his family had received the first letter. And so they received two letters from the Swedish Migration Board within two days.

Aleksander and his family had three weeks to appeal the decision. *We're not just going to accept it,* Aleksander thought. But while the Swedish Migration Board was reviewing the appeal to determine whether the decision should be changed, Aleksander and his family received a deportation decision in their postbox. Which meant that although they could stay in Sweden while they waited for their appeal to be reviewed, it was their responsibility to demonstrate to the Swedish Migration Board that they would, in fact, be leaving Sweden. They needed to arrange for passports and other things necessary for them to return to their country of origin, Russia, and they would need to submit a proof of departure to passport control at a Swedish airport.

For when the deportation decision legally entered into force, Aleksander and his family would have to leave Sweden in the indicated amount of time. If they didn't, the Swedish Migration Board would issue a supervision decision, which would also come to their address in the form of a letter, and they would have to regularly report to the police, in person, while things were being processed.

The permanent residency permit had been rejected because Aleksander had provided a false identity when applying for it— he'd failed to mention the significance of the change of his name to Max Mueller since leaving Russia. It wasn't up to him where they put him and his family now. First, he'd need to be accepted, the appeal needed to go through, and then, through family reunification, his wife and daughter would become eligible through him. But now, a detention decision was sure to be made and of course was. Which meant that Aleksander and his family had to stay at a residency under lock and key, detained, while they awaited their departure. Their futures were no longer up to them. That is to say, there was no way that the refugee family could remain in the room and at the same time be out in the hall locking the door.

It was around this time, after the refugee family had received many letters regarding the Swedish Migration Board's decisions, that Sofya started to act differently. She'd just lie in her bed, not moving, then not speaking.

Sofya had fallen into the syndrome like an animal playing dead in the face of danger. A subtle form of escape. When the family's claim for asylum was refused by the Swedish Migration Board, Dr. Evelyn Volk told Aleksander and his wife that there was nothing either of them could do but focus on their sick child.

Having run after that stern, serious, and haughty bureaucrat and then this stern, serious, and haughty bureaucrat, Aleksander realized there really were no exits, no other paths. He felt lost, really lost—far from all that was friendly and good-natured.

He'd looked for solutions in something new, something outside: a change in society, a new politics. And by taking refuge, his family had become homeless refugees. Helpless, they'd had to hand over all their problems to somebody else, now something else. There were no refugee rations. There was no kind of security or dedicated help. When they became refugees, they gave up their attachment to basic security. Their sense of home ground was illusory. Where they were born wasn't actually any home at all. And because they had no home ground, they were lost souls, so to speak. *Basically*, Aleksander thought, *we are completely lost and confused and, in a sense, pathetic.* They were in a no-man's land in which they were both homeless and groundless. Acknowledging that there was no need for home, or ground, or security was their only expression of freedom left.

Aleksander took refuge in taking no refuge.

If Aleksander's family had received refuge in Sweden, Sofya would have woken up. Since they hadn't been granted admittance, well... it could be months, years even, before she began to recover. And how was he supposed to wait like this? He not only needed refuge from the world but from himself. But where would he find such refuge? Would they be forced underground again? This time for four, seven, maybe even eight years? Sofya was becoming as forbidden inside her own body as the refugee family was forbidden inside the body of Sweden. His daughter was lost, lost inside, and Aleksander, well, Aleksander was still out there but nonetheless as lost as his daughter was. He was outside himself.

Aleksander had been brought back to the uncomfortable edge of dharma. And not in vain did he listen with the new ear he'd discovered deep within himself. And now he knew without any doubt as he sat there, cross-legged, in self-joyous *samādhi*, concentrating only on properly sitting in zazen and nothing but sitting, that something from him had severely dropped off.

Among the online samizdat information that Aleksander had brought into Russia was literature on Buddhism. That was where he'd come across the Sanskrit word *dharma,* which referred to the nature of reality and the ultimate truth of that reality, as taught by the Buddha. He was fascinated by the levels of experience included in the term. "Because in one sense, it seems to be the ultimate fact of who and what we are," Aleksander told his wife as she moved Sofya's legs, bending them at the knee, first the left leg and then the right, to increase the circulation in them and so decrease muscle atrophy. "And in a second sense, dharma is a phenomenon. It's what is so in our lives, whether we like it or not, whether we wish for it or not, whether we expect it or not." Then Aleksander carefully moved Sofya from the bed to her wheelchair. "In its third and fourth senses, dharma is the Buddhist path itself and the Buddhist teachings that lead us along the path. It is precisely this Buddhist path in which Buddhists take refuge, from the first moment on the path to the achievement of full realization that produces buddhas, and it's the dharma that provides the pretext for the *sangha,* the community, and binds it together."

Solspeil

They could do absolutely nothing about the sun's altitude. But the whole history of the town, the dark industrial town of Rjukan, was built on ideas like the *solspeil,* or "sun mirrors." These three giant mirrors on Mount Gaustatoppen reflected sunlight into the valley below, into the dark market square. It wasn't "real sunlight," no, but similar. "Like a spotlight."

The nervous-looking townsfolk who gathered in that beam of Rjukan sun had become afraid to dream of the sun. Those Rjukan-born lived deep in a valley, and for half the year, from late September to mid-March, they lived in shadows. Living in the shadows, their minds became a little bit narrower. Or so Criminal Investigator Quintero reckoned.

He'd been told by the tourist office employee that, a hundred years ago, Norwegian engineer and industrialist Sam Eyde had "harnessed the power of the hundred-metre Rjukanfossen waterfall to generate hydro-electricity in what was, at the time, the world's biggest power plant." And even then, Eyde was considering a suggestion by one of his workers: "a system of mountain-top mirrors to redirect sunlight into the valley below."

These hi-tech sun mirrors, which had begun as something of an art installation, had cost the town five million Norwegian kroner. The Rjukan-born were deeply skeptical and stolidly unimpressed until the project's official opening, which—"complete with shades, sun-loungers, cocktails, and beach volleyball"—made newspaper headlines around the world.

Those Rjukan-born were happy for one day and then realized how really unvital, how really functionless the sun mirrors were. They fulfilled no basic need whatsoever in their lives. Because the only way to cope was to ignore such things as this art installation. To survive here in winter, they had to ignore the possibility of the sun ever reaching them.

The Rjukan-born—whose founder had tamed "the water of the Rjukanfossen waterfall to generate power and build a town, and make a product from air and water that the whole world would buy"—were just surviving, to be sure, through some sound planning and government investment.

Their energetic young mayor had decided the small town could do with some new money. This mayor had said to Criminal Investigator Quintero, at the town hall, with a smile of over-health, that after the launch of the mirrors, he had, for weeks on end, taken calls from one hi-tech company after another. Companies who were interested in relocating to Rjukan, attracted by the cutting-edge technology on view at the top of the mountain.

But these hi-tech companies never did come and probably never would because who would want to seek out that tiny beam of light, that pinpoint of light in the market square? A square "bordered on one side by the library and town hall, and on the other by the tourist office," just to feel the warmth of the winter sun?

The stub of a spent cigarette dangled from one corner of Criminal Investigator Quintero's fleshy pink lips. He stood in the market square, one hand thrust in his pocket, lifting his face to the light. Then he stared—with his half-bitter, half-skeptical grin—northwards, across the square, over the statue of the town's founder and industrialist, Sam Eyde, at the almost sheer mountainside in front of him.

The grey latitudes of Rjukan were clarified and emerging. Surrounding the dark and stony poverty of the town, the peaks comprised a fortress of lead and ash and lichened walls. Grey but for a kind of yellow stoplight, which grew. A malignant disk, that yellow, glass sun.

It was Criminal Investigator Quintero's heavy, lumbering walk and slightly dull manner that seemed to legitimate his being an official in the police's detective department, though he was not.

He'd been hired as a private investigator by the victim's family. He was wearing an old, rather grand, frock coat. A frock coat that made him look old and important.

Criminal Investigator Quintero had traveled from the neurology department at the University of Oslo because he'd been told by the doctor's cognitive neuroscience students that this was where Doctor Philipp Zapf came to do most of his ice climbing. "Between November and April, the Rjukan falls freeze and the ice climbing begins," they said.

"Doctor Zapf will be at the Rjukanfossen waterfall," Criminal Investigator Quintero said with a grunt, in the solitude of his interior forum. He looked just then like an animal with a bullet inside of him. Like he'd survived the hunt but might not survive the coming night.

His hands were freezing, as if his blood had stopped circulating. The coffee at the café on the mountain felt hot across his palms. Criminal Investigator Quintero, having gone to the tourist office to get directions to the Rjukanfossen waterfall, had been carried up into the sunlight by the cable car, Krossobanen.

He realized, with mounting interest and wonder, that it was really a magnificent view out of the café's window. The Nordic sky was suffused with an almost elegiac milkiness.

Within all the logistics and information he'd been inundated with since arriving in Norway, Criminal Investigator Quintero had rather lost sight of the case. He clenched his jaw in stress-induced anger. His thoughts kept returning to his notes, which he now took out of his red folder. They were on the doctor's paradox and what he would do regarding that whole awful mess of a case once the doctor returned from the falls.

These were precious hours and days. Precious ideas, conjectures, hypotheses: *Which will never come to anything legal,* he thought. He couldn't make an arrest, and this, he felt, always made things precarious. Another circumstance would emerge from the painstaking search. It always did.

Criminal Investigator Quintero would subject Doctor Zapf, who had already agreed to be heard and to a questioning. The northern wind was bringing on the night. It was already late, drizzling: nearing that hour of the stomach and the spoon. The doctor would be here soon.

Doctor Zapf told stories to his students. Was known for instantly adapting the plot and focus of these stories to prevent the students' attention from wandering or himself from losing faith in what he had to say. Doctor Zapf did not waver in his tales.

No, Criminal Investigator Quintero thought, *and nor does he waver in his research.* Research on cybernetically intuitive prosthetic interfaces, to be accurate—which, of course, Criminal Investigator Quintero knew absolutely nothing about. But what really counted, in any case, was the constancy of the specifics. He didn't need to know more than the basics of Doctor Zapf's riddle, just the consistency of the case's specifics. He scratched his nose lightly with his thumbnail.

Any reader of difficult philosophy books would experience their own kind of horror at the doctor's philosophy, a philosophy reinforced by public intellectuals who used it as a sort of smoke screen for selling their own inverted self-help books and promoting their own cult of the guru.

Criminal Investigator Quintero despised this kind of fridge-door philosophy.

So, the absolute beginner's introduction to this riddle would be:

— God is dead. God has murdered himself. God's suicide is the extinction of the human species.

That's it, yes, of course: the doctor is a starkly anti-natalist misanthrope who likes to climb mountains and, in the winter months, ice, he concluded then, leaving all his doubts open. Criminal Investigator Quintero didn't need to know much more than this. For instance, it wasn't especially important, that he knew:

— The form of the problem is that, in its most crystalline state, X is tantamount to the negation of X.

Or:

— The problem is at once a problem of logic and an existential problem, even a religious problem. A problem of the contorted logic of this paradox: the height of consciousness is to have revealed the uselessness of consciousness.

But there was some ulterior form of hubris behind the doctor's belief in the explanatory power of his science, something about these neuropsychological explanations that struck Criminal Investigator Quintero as somehow simpleminded.

Criminal Investigator Quintero had to leave his work just then because he was suddenly suffering from a severe headache, what he imagined the doctor would call, pretentiously, if not conceitedly, "a very complex way to the intellectual faculty of attention." No doubt this headache was a result of the exercise in attention to how Doctor Zapf's theory concerned the case.

"Ah, the universe hurts me because my head does." He raised his voice, even shouted a little, and the nervous Rjukan-born took their turns looking first at Criminal Investigator Quintero and then back at the sun that wasn't really the sun.

Eyde built this town just to house his factory workers and now look at it, he thought, gazing out the window once more. *No work. Just the dark. And all they have is the freedom to make their daily trip to the white shadow of those sun mirrors.*

Criminal Investigator Quintero had come a long way to find out just how Doctor Zapf was connected to that awful mess of a case back home in Canada. It appeared that the doctor was involved with more than a science cult here in Norway. He was in fact the founder of United by Hate, a cult leader of a far-right extremist group whose chapters were cropping up throughout Canada. Criminal Investigator Quintero had read about these noxious groups in one of the municipality's little-known magazines. *The* Shambhala Sun*? Yes,* he thought. *Yes, it was released several months back.*

The caregiver, who cared for the victim—whose parents Criminal Investigator Quintero worked for, had gone all the way to Norway for—had fingered some conversations with him in sign language. Through various finger play between the caregiver, the victim, and the investigator, Criminal Investigator Quintero had learned that more than a year had passed since the victim had been taken and returned, unable to speak a word.

"It's all still up there in her head, somewhere in the left hemisphere's language centres," the caregiver had said to Criminal Investigator Quintero, who found it impossible to visualize where these two things met, the grey matter and the essence of language itself. The victim could think clearly, but her mouth and tongue had no memory of the shapes it had formerly made to create sound. Ironically, this didn't prevent her from singing her words in tune with her thoughts. It was part of her therapy to take singing classes, to help her recover from the cocktail of trauma.

The technician who ran the MRI had made some comment about why the victim was the way she was: "Only a neurosurgeon could be this selective. The specific areas that have been lacerated and removed were targeted not only with precision equipment, but also with the precision of a methodology. Let me put it to you another way: there are only a hundred working neurosurgeons worldwide today who could have pulled off an operation like this without killing the patient."

In the procedural brightness of the examination room, the damaged regions in the victim's brain lit up for the technician and the investigator to view. The machine scanned right through the occipital bone, near the spine, on the underside of the skull.

"Mirror-touch synesthesia is rare, but it sounds as if this is what she's been going through. She experiences a sensation in her own body that's similar to a sensation another person might be feeling in that same part of their body. She also has lesions in her Broca's area, which explains her speech aphasia. That should heal with therapy. The global damage, however, might take a considerable amount of time to heal fully."

This is what Criminal Investigator Quintero had to interpret. Careful, frowning, uneasy, he'd written this data on a piece of paper with a stub of pencil then pocketed it. He had some hopes, but not, however, any certainty.

The victim remembered responding to an advertisement posted around her campus at the time, around the neurology department at the University of Oslo, where she was then studying, for a semester abroad. The poster advertised a gynecological study on the correlated effects of sex and pain—that is to say, the experience of pain during sexual intercourse. Payment for participation would take the form of extra credits. She'd been targeted because she'd participated in the dummy experiment, though he couldn't determine any reason she in particular had been targeted, and not someone else like her: a young woman with complete control over her body, her sexuality. Regardless, after she gave them all her information, they knew who she was. *Through and through, they knew who she was,* Criminal Investigator Quintero thought. *Whereas she had known nothing about who they were. They targeted her.*

Just as the victim was transmitting more of her signals with her fingers, motioning toward the caregiver, Criminal Investigator Quintero gave a stupid, cruelly stupid, smile. Not even a smile really—more of a face. It was the face he pulled when he was suffering a migraine.

Criminal Investigator Quintero could see her features again now, in his head. She was a little freckled-face thing. A strange sadness seemed to have filled this woman's face in the moments when he was neither speaking nor looking at the caregiver at the table, only suffering as the reconstruction of events hammered at his temple. It was as if she could feel his head pain.

They added little, the caregiver and the victim, virtually nothing, to what had already been recorded. Time, meanwhile, was pressing.

Criminal Investigator Quintero had been seized, before he came to Norway, by the mania to catch somebody, to not return to her parents empty-handed. An arbitrary and illicit intervention into the doctor's private operations was what he'd suggested to them. But now, he was beginning to understand just how this intervention could spoil the outcome of everything. Because really, he had nothing, and the doctor was smart enough to figure that out right away. And then they would just be two hunters hunting each other like animals.

As a result of this rather withered collection of notes, the greed of the search was gradually being derailed.

After her disappearance, the victim had just appeared, wandering, at random, zombie-like, with something missing in her head. Shortly thereafter, the parents had reunited with their daughter but immediately noticed certain changes, "certain movements…" That was the way they had phrased it to Criminal Investigator Quintero. There were certain movements that were not their daughter's behind her eyes, as if some part of their daughter continued to be somewhere else.

Strange analogies were at work in the brain of Criminal Investigator Quintero. There was no apparent connection, but he would guess that it existed. There was no trail from the club United by Hate to the unknown abductor to those big, shiny, aphasic eyes of the victim to the mountain-climbing doctor. He had limited himself to the formulation of a few hypotheses, one more reasonable than the next. Then a few divergent hypotheses had come about before he suspected at last, having doubled the horns of the dilemma, if not tripled them, that every hypothesis, every deduction, no matter how well constructed, would turn out to have a weak point.

Criminal Investigator Quintero drew a breath mentally with great circumspection. He had to stop this for today. He was getting confused by the throbbing in his temples, which heralded a migraine. The light began to bother him, and he felt nauseous. His coffee cup had already been emptied, refilled, emptied, and again refilled by the barista. *The caffeine could have something to do with the headache, plus the atmospheric pressure at this altitude*, he thought, visibly distressed and taking a larger dose of codeine and acetaminophen, the seasoned pill-popper that he was. He should have ordered decaf. His hypotheses were flickering and dancing in front of his eyes. Absorbed behind a chain of thoughts.

Yet another note on the doctor was there before him, however, this one, unlike the others, seemed to have criminal intent:

— Not only should we cease from procreating, but we should consider the best means by which we as a species can facilitate an extinction that is both inevitable and long overdue.

He couldn't shake the pain. It seemed as if his head were slowly constricting. He clutched it, and then he panicked as a surreal thought came to him: perhaps his skull was shrinking while his brain stayed the same size. The doctor's ideas reverberated in the gathering headache. The air fizzed in and out of focus. An enigmatic expression came to him just then: *I want to live, no matter how.* Criminal Investigator Quintero ruminated and then argued: *If every living thing wants to live, no matter how it does so, the whole of life is then doing all the more harm to itself the more life there is to be lived. Killing us all, only to live.*

By now he was in a cold sweat. *After all*, he thought, *this secret instinct, so independent of all reasoning, that everybody, no, everything, wants to go on living, no matter how, this longing to attain the infinite, however senseless the means, this secret instinct is the deepest, the most insoluble, riddle.* And this riddle would never be understood. People didn't even try to solve it, and for this very reason, the Zapf riddle was a deep one. Nobody wanted to solve it, except the doctor and a few of his students. And, well, maybe Criminal Investigator Quintero, too. For he was utterly lost in the black hole that had opened up inside his head.

He tried to untangle himself from all the serpents of doubt. But Criminal Investigator Quintero was already thinking too much, and once he started thinking, it was hard for him to stop. There was now a gravity, an undertow to being in this time and place, nearly supper on Mount Gaustatoppen, in Rjukan, Norway, and thinking these ideas, these contradictions of contradictions.

The doctor was facilitating an extinction through mediated suicide. United by Hate favoured a new form of discrimination, a discrimination that was not racism, not sexism, not nationalism, not anything of the like, but a disgust and revulsion toward the human species, a disgust toward themselves as a species. Becoming, as they were (as they are!) nothing more than neurocognitive automatons. Uttering unbelievable anathema, void of all common sense. Consuming information on the internet in the cult of themselves, a cult beyond that of the Aryan race. Though they started with this cult, they did not end with it.

For they were reduced. Reduced from a mind to a brain, reduced from that brain to a body, from that body to matter, from matter to dust, from dust to the last fraction of those impersonal atoms, quarks, strings, and bosons that dissolve, dissolve, dissolve the self into so many unnamable and undeterminable particles. Dissolve, dissolve, dissolve until the species is equivalent to the Big Crunch, the ultimate fate of the universe, a dying universe.

And because the death of God was a suicide, there will also be a suicide on the part of matter, since God became the universe and then chose to become matter. Flesh. Even Christ lost in the fight against matter. So the decaying body of God is really as much a part of the universe of matter as it is the consciousness of the human species. Because if immortals are mortal and mortals immortal, if the life of one is the death of the other, and the death of one is the life of the other, then not only do all the gods die a death greater than death itself, but so do all the...

Through his blurred eyesight, his eye in the void, Criminal Investigator Quintero looked down at the apparition of the sun—a faint, ephemeral sphere in the Rjukan dark. Because of its glowing halo, it looked very much like the superheated gas captured over a period of ten days by the Event Horizon Telescope. This black hole, six and a half billion times bigger than the sun and located at the centre of the galaxy Messier 87, fifty-five million light years away, was the first black hole to ever have its picture—direct visual evidence of its existence—taken.

That is to say, Criminal Investigator Quintero's migraine made his vision about as clear as that picture of the black hole—a black hole that was not millions of light years away but right here, down in the Rjukan square itself, a square "bordered on one side by the library and town hall, and on the other by the tourist office." The direct visual evidence of its existence, beyond his hypothesizing, was there at the centre of this blotted-out town square, the centre of dark Rjukan.

And it was the doctor, Doctor Philipp Zapf, that was this black hole. Criminal Investigator Quintero saw this black hole as he descended from the café summit in the Krossobanen.

He knew that he would never reach the centre of this black hole of a doctor, or what physicists called the singularity, the point where extremely large amounts of matter are crushed into an infinitely small amount of space. For a maddening enigma lies at the point where every star dies.

He knew only that there was the doctor, the image of the doctor, that his eyes had received him—that much he'd decided himself. His head had accepted a distorted picture. He lived with this picture, and now he was supposed to go on with it. There was just this conclusion left, which he muttered to no one in particular.

United by Hate

There's something satisfying about reading the last paragraph of a story first. So that's how this story is going to start.

The final paragraph of my long-form investigative journalism piece, titled "Seen Through the White," was this: *Sometimes to prove the obvious, you must assume the doubtful. For everywhere, certainty is indistinguishable from doubt, truth from error—that which is not distinguishable is a necessary insight.*

This piece of journalism didn't follow a linear structure, and neither did the process of writing it. Because racism is abstract.

When you're covering the fallout of an enormity the likes of which I was working on for two years—which required taking on the role of investigator on my own—journalism simply can't be as straightforward as you might like it to be. No. I know now that I couldn't have told it any other way. But maybe this was a result of my inability to deal with the unexpected consequences and the omissions that had to be made. Maybe I knew the ending enough only to not recognize it when I returned to it in my own way.

It's racist to say that art, or any form of expression for that matter, is dead. Journalism is alive and well, as is poetry, which has never been more involved, never more folk. Death prevents people like us, minorities, from reframing the narrative. But even death must die.

We all could have seen it coming. Ah, if only our fathers were our sons, it might have been different. The news industry failed to believe that investing in the internet was a good idea. They thought that no one would ever stop needing news that was told in a truthful, objective manner. That seems silly now, given that the leading career path of a journalist involves marketing and that the best kind of marketing is misinformation.

A team of us were fortunate enough to be given a year-by-year contract to investigate the emergence of fake news, to spotlight the rise and fall of far-right media in Canada. I say fortunate because until then I'd been doing nothing but freelance work and internships that didn't pay much, if anything at all. This contract meant that I'd be interviewing people I didn't even know existed before the American election. It would take me into the backwaters of anti-liberal thought—a place I'd never expected myself to go.

Because I'm what some call "white-passing" (my father being a white man and my mother a Black woman), and because I've always appeared boyish, all I had to do was shave my Afro hair, tape down my breasts, and become a neo-Nazi fan of the group United by Hate.

We've become skilled in selectively ignoring the world. A new ignorance is on the horizon, an ignorance born not of a lack of knowledge but of too much knowledge; too much data, too many theories, too little time. The more we know, the less we know.

Designated for very specific targets, millions of ads create revenue off subliminal content as reader attention shifts from page to page, the click-throughs leaving little to no trace in the whirlpool of the internet, just temporary sparks seen flickering on the screen.

And according to Parmenides, seeing is the same as being.

This is a story about post-truth and the propaganda that brought an end to politics; this is a story about post-reality and the propaganda that brought an end to reality. This was the expectation I intended to live up to as I wrote.

Go further.

Reasons are often given through non-reasons. This is what drives the nonsense. This is how havoc spreads: mass killings, single-assailant hate crimes, and, even more often, suspected anti-establishment cults, attempting to establish minimum order in the disorder, which ranged anywhere from attempted assassinations to fire-bombings and shooting sprees.

"The highest violence," one apprehended gunman said, to the behavioural science unit of the Halifax Regional Police, "is order itself."

*

United by Hate claims to be an old club deleted long ago, even though the page was seemingly created just two weeks prior to my joining them. Its membership numbers remain statistically minor. They have only several hundred online followers, mostly visitors from other far-right groups across the internet.

Outwardly, UBH members present themselves as invested in charitable work. They give out pizza to the homeless, praise veterans, and pick up litter: entry-level acts of kindness that mostly serve to downplay their extremist beliefs.

The first iteration of UBH in Canada had many obvious ties to neo-Nazism, but the network splintered after a year or so, over disagreements about whether to remain loyal to Norway. Before it was shuttered, Nova Scotia's UBH chapter proudly claimed on its website that it was the first to be "Norway approved."

"I don't want to fight the racist finger-pointing anymore," the president of UBH says to me, with a smile of omnipotent hatred. A president who was convicted for a racially motivated assault only a decade ago and was more recently barred from local coffee shops for his rants against Syrian refugees and people of the Islamic faith. "I want to have a club that folks can trust and rely on. Strictly dedicated to charitable work. But we aren't afraid of using violence to achieve objectives. We will announce our beliefs about another race. This is our future. We won't back down. We will stand up. We will be heard."

There's pride in his words, as well as sorrow and distrust. And, well, these three things together make a bad sound. He raises his bloodshot, bestial eyes to the heavens, as if to invoke the approval of the gods of his race. Then he takes another shot of brown whisky water from his tumbler.

At the president's side is a recruiter, high up in the skinhead movement. He wears an image of the UBH logo over a skull and pistols flanked by *kafir*, the Arabic word for "infidel," written in both languages. I speak and listen through the white side of my face, paternal, pensive, inviting: as welcoming as a trap.

We're at a local bar, Charles, which used to be the clubhouse of a white supremacy group in the seventies but is now the main hangout for UBH members when they aren't patrolling the streets. For years now, the members of UBH have performed theatrical rituals, which they claim are "for Nordic tourists."

Whether there's physical violence or not, the street patrols themselves are a form of violence. A form of intimidation. Intended to keep people silent. From coast to coast, there has been an increase in the number of these far-right extremist groups. Over a hundred now exist. The largely white law enforcement agencies are aware, but, of course, not actively investigating them.

It's unlikely that United by Hate, or any other group, will coordinate a planned attack. Ultimately, the root cause of the "lone wolf" attacks is hate propaganda. A single soldier or UBH fan becomes radicalized and carries out the group's message to deadly result.

Since 9/11, white supremacists and other far-right extremists have killed more people in North America than any other category of terrorist. It's gotten to the point that I'm afraid that, if I publish the story, my mother, with whom I live, might find a bomb in the mail that was intended for that journalist who was speaking out.

Because violence is never intended to hurt more than the target, but it always does.

There was a Swiss bio-politician in Russia, Töm Tscharner, who studied the theory of autopoietic social systems: a theory that systems are capable of reproducing and maintaining themselves independent of their parts. In his seminal work, *The Autopoietic Society,* Töm Tscharner argues that this not only applies to society—the theory being that a society has everything it needs to run on its own and requires limited or no human intervention—but to everything that can be closed off somewhere deep in its essence. All things are systemic beings in themselves.

Töm Tscharner wanted to run social experiments to confirm this. In his lifetime, the necessary computational ability to do so was limited, if not nonexistent, so it remained purely speculative. At that time, it was common for theories in the realm of the social sciences to advance farther than the technology that would give them the necessary empirical support. Now that the internet's social technology is so widespread, his students are ready to pick up where their founder's speculative thought left off.

Töm Tscharner's legacy team has prepared an algorithm that, when applied to the internet, is designed to train individuals to increase their autopoietic abilities through repeated web usage. In order to do this, a person must be able to interpret everything as a result of their individualistic ideologies; they must train their behaviour to be unpredictable to others. Weaponize their identities. Once completely insulated, the individual can insulate others by means of the same algorithm. Effectively creating an arms race. Here, conspiracy reinforces conspiracy. What makes this different from regular ideologies is the intensity with which the algorithm works on the individual post-ideologically.

As one of the more technical papers on the subject would have it: "Users of the internet do not explore how different people perceive the internet but rather how the internet perceives them as it becomes more of a force in their everyday lives."

The hypothesis is that these test subjects will form the basic unit of a culture—a culture that often shares in a collective hallucination brought on by the stress of being the outgroup of the larger sample, the greater culture, which they will choose to abandon. In conclusion, their absence will not impede the continued function of either system.

Why is this a useful theory? Because, if it's true, the progressive leap to an entirely new social paradigm will bring the kind of prosperity, and equally opposite disparity, that would never fully occur in a non-codependent system. Basically, for society to progress, it needs no people; and for people to progress, they need no society. This is the conflict, the contradiction, and the conundrum.

In Töm Tscharner's own famous words, "Absolute miscommunication is a necessary truth."

It's been a year, and I've lost control of my story. I still don't know how I should tell it. My colleagues, who are covering other angles of the same story, don't seem to have reached the conclusions I've drawn. Maybe they picked a side too early. I'm still waiting to start writing.

"I might disappear for a while," I tell my colleagues in the lunch lounge of the Shambhala Sun Foundation, where I work with the editorial group on their bimonthly magazine. We're united by compassion, but I'm too bottled up to explain the constant inner conversation I've been having with myself to the team right now. Explaining myself would require more energy than I have, and they would only spout the self-help advice that I've already read in their reprinted articles. I have to keep on running with the story. So, instead, I offer myself *metta*. I gently repeat the simple phrases:

May I be free from danger.
May I have mental happiness.
May I have physical happiness.
May I have ease of well-being.

The children of my mixed-income housing development smile and wave at me. They play their games in the tree hollows, whose cavities were sealed by the people who lived in the area before it was gentrified. These trees survived the axe because baked bricks were fitted into the holes. Now there are no bricks. They have been removed by the city, and again the sapwood gathers bacteria and fungus in its watery bole.

Disease spreads.

I'm smoking a cheap cigarette at the little writing desk near the balcony window, the balcony I share with my neighbours in this housing development. The children wonder who I am when they see me, the woman whose head is sometimes crowned with black braids that fade into a vivid purple ombré, and who other times dresses like a neo-Nazi, has no hair to speak of, and has bleached white eyebrows. They should wonder. They have every reason to wonder.

The building itself is the result of a reparation effort undertaken by the municipality's council of city planners and urban designers, who came together to provide subsidized housing for anyone capable of drawing up their genealogical tree on a piece of bureaucratized paper, from the roots of indentured servitude up. Most had ties to the historic diaspora, runaway American slaves whose harbourside community was demolished overnight by the municipal government for industrial use of the land. They still had a church. I was told that if I wanted to know my roots, I should go to this church.

The minister there had me stand before the congregation and declare my relatives. I said: "My name is Valencia Hendriks, but Smith was my slave name." And like that, a snap of the fingers and those church people identified me. Who knew religion could be more useful than the internet.

The Black community represents five percent of the population of these new constructions. Another four percent went to refugees: Muslims and Syrians. Then, one percent of the total ten percent, equivalent to about eight apartment houses, went to youth who have severe physical disabilities.

One of these eight youths is my neighbour. She's twenty-eight years old, and although she doesn't need somebody watching her twenty-four hours a day, somebody always needs to be there for her.

"Before this, she was warehoused at a nursing home, living with people in their eighties and nineties. The ones who say, 'Somebody kill me, please.'"

I accepted the fingered cigarette from the caregiver with a kind of restrained coldness. We were on the shared balcony when she told me something that made me think that this woman, my neighbour, was somehow involved in my investigative piece. The mystery only deepened and broadened, became more elusive, infinitely complex, impossible to prove.

"Her case is rather open-handed, actually. The family wouldn't stop pressuring the police department to look into it further, and when the police did nothing, they sent a private investigator all the way to Norway. Norway of all places! I don't know what he'd be doing there. But anyway, the girl's lucky to have a family who can pay for her to live independently with care support. I figure it costs them ten thousand dollars a year. Otherwise, she would have been put on a waiting list with a thousand other people in her position."

The ring of smoke from our cigarettes lingered above and then drifted toward the improbable needs of a tomorrow where neither bread, nor power, nor water was guaranteed.

Lost Inside

Aaden's lawyer didn't know why Aaden was being transported inside an armoured police vehicle. He'd already completed his four years in segregation. But he wasn't being released yet. He was being moved from a prison in New Brunswick to an immigration detention centre in Toronto. There would be a detention review hearing and then a deportation hearing and Aaden's lawyer would challenge the detention order and then both Aaden and his lawyer would challenge the deportation order in federal court. But, well, of course, it would really be up to the Canadian government to stop it from happening. Because the case was complicated. That is, being detained on immigration grounds.

Aaden was nervous about the upcoming deportation proceedings. Not only was he not a Canadian citizen, but he'd also committed a crime: aggravated assault. And now, so he was told, many people who were Canadian citizens wanted him to be deported to Somalia, a country he knew nothing about, having been only six years old when he arrived in Nova Scotia. Although he was a Somalian refugee, he'd spent most of his life in Canada. He was twenty-four years old now, and he hadn't known that he wasn't a Canadian citizen until he was charged with aggravated assault. No one had told him he wasn't, not even after he'd lived in more than two dozen foster homes. No legal guardian had told him he was a child without citizenship. Nobody had told him that he should be a Canadian citizen but wasn't. Not after he'd been carded, time and again, by the police. Because after living in a place with twenty, thirty, forty messed-up kids who'd gone through traumatic experiences and had no parental guidance, he realized that they were all there just to live. And that was about it. Left to be influenced by themselves and their environment. Nobody looked at the root of the problem—at how he'd grown up without guidance and all he'd had to reflect on were the experiences of those other kids in their mental hells.

His life was now at risk. Somalia was war-torn. And yet, here he was inside this armoured police vehicle, as though he were back in prison. A double punishment. An armoured door had opened at the rear of the vehicle like a heavy bank vault. The squat cube was empty when he was placed in it. It was bare, crude, with something violently uninhabitable about it. And it remained locked all day long. All through the twelve-hour trip from New Brunswick to Toronto, only a brutal shaft of light from a narrow window cut through the gloom. The feeling of confinement became oppressive. The sensation of the hermetic block sealed around him, sealed the floor to the walls, the walls to the ceiling; floor, walls, ceiling, and door, all made of brand-new galvanized steel. It was hard to reconcile what he saw with the structure's overall dimensions. *Someone ought to put up some labels reading top and bottom*, he thought.

The federal government didn't look at the conditions in Somalia. They didn't look at Aaden's experience in care, and they didn't look at the reasons why Aaden hadn't become a Canadian citizen. But someone had—two people, in fact. They'd been there to hear his story while he was in prison. And they'd be there to meet him in Toronto, so they said. They'd confronted the prime minister about the case. And they'd taken his sister to the town hall meeting and told her what to ask and how to ask it—namely, why the prime minister was deporting her brother. And of course, when the prime minister had spoken, he'd spoken not only for everyone in the room, but also for all people across the country, saying that when they—the prime minister, everyone who was in the room, and all of the country outside the room—saw how the care system had failed him, saw how the challenges he faced had impacted him, they also saw the real challenges being faced in the system. However, the prime minister had said, any time a deportation order was issued, it was done with a great deal of care, and while the prime minister couldn't speak specifically to Aaden's case, he believed that no final decision had been made.

This was a political answer. And Aaden was not a political question. It didn't help him, Aaden, the person sitting in an armoured police vehicle, not knowing up from down, though he appreciated that the prime minister had answered at all, even if just to provide a political answer to a political question.

But right now, Aaden wasn't a political entity but a human being. Really, it didn't help him or the other kids in his situation, the twenty, thirty, forty messed-up kids who'd soon be in this exact spot. The criminal justice system, child welfare, and immigration: all were collecting data, data, and more data. Data disaggregated by race and so crossing multiple systems, particularly anti-indigenous and anti-black systems. And, sure, the government might back away after he'd been brought across the nation to Toronto. They might drop the deportation and stop everything. But he wasn't going to stop being Black in Canada. No, he wasn't going to stop being Black in Canada. He had been, was now, and forever would be this Black human being.

The Weight of Skin

"Skin isn't usually thought of as an organ, but it is the largest one. It includes everything that covers the body. The nails on feet and hands, the hair on the body and head, the calluses that form wherever contact is made most, and the genitals where contact is made least. It even has an average weight—most adults wear more than twenty pounds wherever they go. There is, however, something that the facts don't figure.

"My skin is heavier than yours. I don't mean objectively. If you were to take me and skin me alive, you would prove I was lying when I said 'My skin is heavier.' Once on the scale, it would likely arrive at a number just above twenty pounds. But that is an object's weight. That object you weigh on your scale is not me.

"If you skinned me alive, making sure to rip off my nails from their beds and scalp my hair from below their roots, I would be screaming that my skin is heavier than yours. If you kept me alive long enough to compare my weight, before and after being removed from my object, I would still be screaming after, because my largest organ is in your well-trained hands, like the possessive object it has always been to you.

"But now, what is it that screams before you? How deep will you go to find where the screaming comes from? Will you look at all? Will you gather up all the people claiming heavier skin and do the same as you did to me, so that we can all hear the victims scream over and over again?

"You invented this object to put something between you and me, and objectively, you succeeded. But my heaviness is the subject, and my subject is a scar. It's a twisted white scar that runs from me to you. If you skin me alive to show that we are equal, only to hear me scream that my skin weighs the same as yours, you will see that the deeper you go, the whiter the scars become. Even if your skin is light."

Her last night as poet laureate was different. It had a special electric quality to it. Years of being the token, of weekly slots placed at bars and fundraisers and government-sponsored functions, such as this one, were mere cadavers to the real thing, the real body electric.

After hearing the poem, the people with the light skin in the room waited for a response. The people with the heavy skin in the room smiled on the inside, and if there were more of them, they would have cause to acknowledge this as victory. Poet laureates carry their heaviness alone, because they don't perform for heavy crowds. They perform for light crowds.

Our poet laureate was bravest when she looked them in the eyes, and sometimes she invaded the audience's comfort zone, and not only with her poetry. They clapped anyway. Hearing the words but never really understanding what the poet was saying. The gesture left the impression of an ovation, but they clapped without the sound of hands coming together.

Once the reading is over, what itches at their minds is the guilt they think they should have more of. They praise her for her gift of helping them understand that guilt. They've made contact with the temperate surface of something other than them, and that's enough to feel good. But the guilt never really is guilt, just some lesser form of hatred.

After the event, she left in her wake a dreadful overawe. The memorized lines receded into the shell of her temporal lobe, like a slimy thing that you can't hold on to, patiently waiting to unfurl and be the second tongue of her mouth to speak again. Tonight, she recited the ones she always did, the one about the prisoners in their cages, growing sicker by the day, then another on the irony of waiting for reparations that never come from those with the most celebrated of debts. This last recitation, though, this was something she wouldn't have thought she could do, until tonight.

She was usually too nervous, and when she was too nervous, she forgot the lines.

* * *

"It was the pain that saved us..."

M.K___ listens through the tiny radios embedded in her ears as she waits at a terminal to transfer to the connector bus en route to Halifax. 'Transit is horrible in this city,' she thinks, 'they should be paying me to take it.'

When the bus finally arrives she mills in and takes a seat. The voices she is plugged into shake and quiver with the sound of anguish, her ears scabbed over by earbuds.

She has been following coverage on the inquiry into the missing and murdered Indigenous women. Community consultations were featured in a podcast. Already hearing clips from five out of the ten provinces, the inquiry was well underway.

It often feels like change, but it isn't. She knows better now. The victims would go on and on with their suffering and, in the eyes of the government, they would still be denoted as victims.

The night before, M.K___ had gone to the last performance of the province's poet laureate. It was powerful. She smiled again, inwardly, remembering the ambiguousness of the crowd's reaction.

Her own position was precarious. Recently, she spoke out against Islamophobia, and an unjust celebration of violent colonial history. As a student activist, she often spoke out, with distressing but manageable repercussions. This time, however, there was a lash-back to her post. It was the country's sesquicentennial anniversary.

'North American history is full of a genocidal momentum that has not been slowed, but curbed. I refuse to celebrate a national moment that, if not approving of this, willingly ignores the multi-tier offense it is to the people that have been colonized, and the groups that are still being racially and sexually subjugated. White fragility? Reverse racism? How can there be such things? When you experience what I experience, then you can complain to me about it! Until then, fuck you all and your white privilege!'

The comments streamed in, and after the election of a neo-fascist demagogue across the border, white pride was on the rise. The comments were vulgar, reactionary and male, blurring the lines between hatred, sexual violence, and inverted guilt—pride. She could imagine them typing the error laden threats, with every misspelled word indicating the blood from their brain was in their stiffened dicks, throbbing with rape-lust and warping their enemy into an inhuman object.

@███████ 9:52 AM
'...Let your brown tears lub the fat white cock that I will be fucking your little muslim pussy with you hypocritical bitch!...'

@███ 10:34 AM
'...go back to the shit country where you came from you ugly drty whore...'

@█████████ 11:11 AM
'...I am proud of my white heritage and if I have to kill you to set an example, I will! And I am not the only one there is, WE are MANY...'

As she was notified of them, she felt the terror of being a woman, the fear of being born coloured, and the anxiety of being human.

They had no idea that she was born and raised in their country, they just pointed and fired. As her mobile phone vibrated, and her virtual identity was lynched by clicks and angry fingers against keyboards, she looked at the other people, mostly students that filed onto the university bus. They were tapping away at the glass screens in their palms, and she did not trust them because to her, they all looked the same, because to her, they were all anonymous threats that had the potential to be real.

* * *

The mediocre white man was white in every way. He did not feel the same invisible turbulence of outrage that was in the flight path of those that looked like him, but he wasn't racist. He felt safe as long as this was his position.

He would repeat to himself, *Hold your peace and ask no dangerous questions, hold your peace....*

But there were some things that the alt-right were not wrong about. Despite all his cognitive dissonance on the topic, he had to admit he was underemployed, and he was losing his historical narrative. When he said that Black Lives Matter, which he was neither proud of nor ashamed of, he was going against his own people. He may not have been mixed in ethnicity, but his feelings certainly were.

Then, again, he would repeat to himself, *Don't think, for what you think happens. Don't think...*

He first heard the Proud Boys chant 'white lives matter' at a protest. A statue of a murderer and the founder of the city stood over him as people demanded the immediate removal of a historic monument. A pang for belongingness agitated whatever resolve he had gained against the dangerous questions. Why was it that Black life mattering meant white life not mattering, and vice versa?

The statue was concealed in a black tarp and at its base support was a mass of people. Some of them held burning herbs, sage, and juniper in the air, the fumes smudging the bad spirits away. All kinds of speakers took the podium—activists, and later on, politicians. Farther out, just beyond the crowd of protesters, the counter-group, the alt-right, were also gathering in numbers.

The former poet laureate took the mic, and she made it her intention to point them out, because up until then, they were simply being ignored. She was supposed to introduce the new poet to the public eye, but instead she took an opportunity to recite a final poem, dedicated to the Proud Boys. She had said it once before, on the night of the centennial.

The mediocre white man had never heard anything like it. It was as though she had stabbed herself with a knife, twisted it, and, as if by way of some voodoo running through them, she dragged it from her in a jagged line, to him.

When she was finished, the protesters, having heard the intention behind the poem, turned on the Proud Boys. Now punctured by the sharpness of her verse, the Proud Boys yelled a few hurtful words, and moved on to avoid a fight, tails between their legs.

After the ruckus, the former poet laureate gestured toward an Indigenous woman and handed her the mic. The new poet laureate took her place in front of the crowd: "These red dresses that hang from the branches of these trees represent the missing and murdered among us..."

The scarlet dresses hung on wire hangers, like tree-climbing children swaying and swinging from the boughs—only their arms and legs were missing.

He left the protest early. In one motion he opened the door to his car and turned the ignition. He drove without thinking, and the mediocre white man had taken the same route as the Proud Boys. He would have never noticed, except a plea for help stole his attention from the wheel.

He thought he recognized the woman—she wore a khimar, and looked similar to the one featured on the cover of a local newspaper. He couldn't remember which, or what the article was about. What he did remember, however, was that in that picture she had looked fierce, an ominous red zone with smoke billowing behind her. The background that the photographer used somehow enhanced her courage and determination to what was almost revolutionary. But here, in the flesh, she just looked like an average woman, on her way somewhere, possibly a late arriver to the protest.

The horde of Proud Boys surrounding her, all in military uniform, with their hair shaved close to their heads, started up with their act again—only now the numbers were uneven, weighed to their advantage. They told her what she was to them. Grabbed her. Pulled her down and into the street, into the rays of midday-light. They made it more exceptionally real than the mediocre white man could process through the tempered glass of his windshield.

He watched as the situation escalated, worsened, as the boys brutalized her with heavy army boots and yelled out blunt demands at the top of their lungs, as if the street had become the protest. He was so far lost in his own indecision that, even when they began ripping off her khimar, he could only fail to understand the sense of urgency that the situation called for, failed to see that she was looking at his vehicle, asking for whoever was inside to see that her life mattered more than his protection. His wired fight-or-flight response was intensified by the tonnes of vehicle that was both a weapon for him, and security from the events just outside; he could never be hurt within this privileged bubble, as long as he remained uninvolved.

He would have lost nothing if he pretended to plow into the assaulters, to scare them off anonymously with a honk of the horn. The news was full of motorist terrorism anyway. Why couldn't he use it for good? But anonymity is prone to cowardice, and little fears become lesser evils when given the opportunity to escape into mediocrity.

Mediocrity is an invisible monster, and at the stop sign, he steered the car up the street, in the opposite direction, and listened to the words that now defined him, not by his choice not to act, but because of his choice not to choose. "...We want our country back! We want our jobs back! We want our women back! We want our pride back! We want our lives back..."

Looking into the side view mirror, as if once removed from not just this crime, but every crime he would ever commit, he thought of his best intentions, reading and re-reading the warning:

OBJECTS IN MIRROR ARE CLOSER THAN THEY APPEAR.

Empty Comforts

Whenever she had heart palpitations, she drove the ring road. It was how she managed to contain the pain, to keep it from growing any more intense. The pain was getting so powerful that she refused to acknowledge it was hers. And it descended on her so swiftly that it made her suddenly aware. Here she sat. Here she was, driving. Though she was going nowhere fast, she was at least somewhere when on the ring road.

She had needed to go through the city centre for over a quarter of a century. Back then, her commute was very different. All around her the roar, rumble, thundering of business traffic; on the left and on the right, above and below. Her car crawled through the guts of the city. Her hands moved over other worlds as she scrolled through her phone. And now here she sat. Here she was, driving, no longer in the middle of the city but on its outskirts, in a vehicle that was newly leased but of the same make as she'd had then.

She'd been laid off from the oil and gas company with a severance package, rendering all her years of accumulated stock useless. On top of this, the symptomatic grief and loneliness she felt after her adult children had left home, first one and then the other, compounded her suffering. She managed to find some solace in the many tax-deductible luxury items of promotional merchandise still bearing the obsolete logo of her former employer—anything from oil skin jackets and engraved pens to knife block sets and blankets—which comforted her about as much as a nest of bright, egg-shaped objects might have comforted a raven.

The company had made the best recruiters available to her, and had even given her an option to interview at the new company. She'd declined, knowing it was a corral office setup, and she despised corral office setups, which she'd worked in for years.

So she took a year off, because who wouldn't? She took a year off to find new work but nothing came. And she was afraid nothing would ever come again in this city.

But work did come again: work at cannabis and IT companies, at law firms and financial institutes, at design agencies and municipal offices. The recruiter hadn't really understood her, not being a recruiter specializing in accountants. Mostly the recruiter didn't understand why she had so much experience, thirty or more years to be exact, and no designation: "You're not a CA? Not a CPA either?"

No: just an accountant with experience, who, in the economy that had taken a turn for the worst, found herself out of respectable work. Unrespectable work would always be available to her, of course. No matter what their designation, accountants were never unwanted of their profession. Because there was always money to be counted.

It had been three months since she started at the textile company, and in those three months, she'd found that every single link to the person she'd been hired to replace revealed a most egregious error. Every single item in the accounts book was erroneous. Every single item in the balance sheet was erroneous. Every single item in the corrections, alterations, clarifications, revisions. Nothing but errors, errors upon errors. She often found letters where numerical signs should have been, or descriptions that contained both words and numbers. Only one thing comforted her: the feeling that her real work experience had indeed existed once upon a time, and that this experience would help her get away from all this. Because this wasn't real work. It was cleanup work, work that software could do competently, almost automatically, not the work of an oil-and-gas accountant who had steadily earned an income that was well above the happiness salary, plus benefits.

Away, get away. This had been her immediate thought after passing her assessment for the role at the textile company that specialized in manufacturing blinds. But not even the courage to think this was throbbing inside her anymore. Nothing like that was throbbing inside her now. Nothing but her own cold, hollow heart.

She drove in silence.

She caught sight of the rows of tumbled-down suburban buildings with their crumbling stucco forms and fading beige vinyl, the colour of tedium. These rows of houses, these shrines of suburbicarian devotion, were heaped upon each other on the hills curving along the bends in the ring road. This was already enough, this first hour. A glimpse of the countryside over a suburban wall didn't give her any sense of freedom. Just more dread.

The person she'd replaced had died. Not only had he died, but he'd died before he finished his contract with the small private company as the one and only accountant. He wasn't even full-time, and had no assistant to speak of.

"Only three months ago," the intern had told her. "He was sitting at his ancient desk—now your desk." A desk with, regrettably, no windows near it, unlike the desk she'd worked at previously, in the hundred-storey building.

"He was a man," so the intern recounted to her coworker, "this Michael Fredette, troubled by obscure ailments, and he had died working between ailments. He was dull, old, and sweaty, with dirty shoes. His hair was always flattened from his hat, revealing an incipient baldness. His shirt bore horrible coffee stains, and he wasn't at all sure of himself—so much so that he was a curmudgeon with the staff. This Michael Fredette, after pretending to search in one of his jacket pockets for a packet of cigarettes, would leave to buy another carton and would then smoke at regular intervals a few feet away from the garbage bin until he needed to buy another packet."

The staff had seen his death coming long before death had actually come to take him, suddenly, by way of an aneurysm in the brain. He had gone blind near the end, which was evident in the state of the books.

"In fact, he'd been ill for years," the intern had explained, though the accountant was very busy and had no time for small talk. But they couldn't just fire him because he was sick, no—he'd done contract work there for nearly a decade. That wouldn't have been right. So the office staff agreed to keep him on part-time right to the very end. "Right here, in this very desk—now your desk." And although he was absolutely unfit for the job, at least he performed the task to which he was condemned.

It was only when she had the accounts book lying open before her eyes that the accountant realized she wouldn't be working over lunch for months, but for months and months. Possibly half a decade was wrong. At least half a decade was wrong. Somebody would have to reconcile each off-balanced year, from the first misentry to the last—*at a rate of a month for each year, no quicker being possible*, she thought—while still keeping up with the daily accounting.

No, it would not be her, definitely not her. Someone else would have to consolidate this without her. Someone else would have to draw up the accounts and make a loss. She would add up the figures and then pass on to something better, that is, if her contract would allow it.

The thick page of the ledger made a crisp, tremulous sound as she, a clerical nobody, an accountant in a fabric warehouse, a textile company, checked some figures. Forever between balance sheets. Monotonous and necessary, commanding and unknowable.

There certainly had been nothing surprising in her being chosen for the job, though it would have been gratifying to know that it was her well-known perfectionism, endless perseverance, and unflinching work ethic that had convinced her boss of her indisputable rightness for the job. A boss always ready with some inappropriate joke and whose soul was out of touch with the universe. And an office manager whose inoffensive jokes offended the whole universe. They left the office together around six but on the odd day would leave at five for some vague business outside the office and then come back, to the evident surprise of the other employees.

"Back already?"

"Yes, back already." Behind in their work but nevertheless cheered by their leaving and coming back, their mental holiday.

Facing the accountant on the sloping desk were the large pages of the heavy accounts ledger. She drew up a balance sheet on what felt like the back of her insomnia, looked with weary eyes at the two white pages, filled with her careful numbers recording the company's results, filled with the names of fabrics and various sums of money, filled with blank pages, ruled lines, and letters. She wrote down the names of fabrics she didn't know. She observed the half-written page of her previous work and, although she felt drowsy, saw she'd made no mistake. She noted her rather unlovely writing.

The stoop-shouldered office manager, not far from her, in fact directly behind her, wrote out bills, while the accountant covered up the company's irreparable past. Across the laborious futility of each identical day she faultlessly wrote a number or a sum.

If I left them all tomorrow, what else would I do? she thought, distracted from her debit and credit column. *Because I would have to do something. And what suit would I wear? Because I would have to wear another suit.*

Another lost day drew to an end. The office was now lit by a black electricity. The accountant had finished her work but didn't want to move. Then, slowly, her hand closed the book, shutting it completely, and she raised her eyes, weary with unshed tears. She had sensed the quiet. It seemed as if the world had ended in this squalid office of hers. The sound of dishes being placed in the staff sink, water running in that sink, emphasized, rather than interrupted, this absolute absence of sound, this vacuity.

Here she was, at this ancient desk—now her desk—demanding answers; but no one had answers. No one knew what they did, no one knew what they wanted, no one knew what they knew.

With enormous effort she rose only to find that she seemed to be carrying the chair with her. She armed the security system with the security code and hastily locked the place up. Then she walked along the poverty of the Calgary streets that separated the rooms of her house from those of her office and did so as if she were still seated in a chair, her attentive mind still filled with the inertia of a body in repose. The streets frequently provoked physical disgust in her. The grubby everydayness of life, the monotonous squalor of these beggarly lives that ran parallel to her own.

At the abandoned station, the previous train had left half an hour ago, and the next was yet to arrive. Between stations, people were talking about other people. She rested on a bench and took off her black business shoes, which had been rubbing against a sore.

The Suburban Line train made its slow way down the avenues. The flash of bright steel above the doors in the middle of each car, the articulated arms of the pantograph, the cables of the catenary suddenly blue with a metallic light. It came to a stop at the station. A man with his pants rolled up to his knees looked at her as he would have looked at anyone in particular. As the city train departed the densely built-up areas and made its way past the scarce houses on the slopes of the hills at the outer edge of the city, she noted that the trees, lined up along the avenues, had nothing to do with all this, this avalanche of houses.

The accountant couldn't even entertain the idea of retirement for years. When a person with her experience got a short-term contract like this one, it was inevitable how things would go: she would become absolutely unfit for any future long-term contracts. In the eyes of the recruiting agency, she would have a reputation for taking only short-term contracts from here on out, *ad infinitum.*

The train reached her stop. She lifted herself up.

"An impossible task," she told her husband, the barber, after she got in the car. He had been waiting for her in the rotting parkade of the train station, a horribly filthy station because everyone spit on the ground here, and that's why it had felt so sticky as her heels *click-clacked* over the cement.

"They want an impossible task from me and I can't give them what they want," she said to her husband, the barber. The barber who, from day to evening, was the voice behind the towel. The barber who all day told stories seamlessly and so had no more energy when the lights went off in the barber shop. The barber who was her husband, her lover, her companion, her hands for everything practical, her chauffeur, her soul. The barber who obsequiously nodded his enormous head and answered flatly, and then rolled down his window and spit on the decaying cement.

"Not only is the task impossible but so are the people," the accountant said to her husband, the barber, as they bagged their own groceries. Then they walked to their vehicle with a number of heavy shopping bags hooked over their bent fingers and loaded the banana boxes already in the trunk.

"The office manager, who's completely oblivious, spent an entire month convincing the entire office to put down money on what he claimed was a sure bet through one of those online gambling services. He told us that 'life's biggest lottery prize goes only to those who happen to buy tickets.'

"Of course, that *guaranteed* return amounted to nothing," the accountant said to her husband, the barber, as they entered their house through the detached garage, having briefly disremembered what they'd been talking about, "so you might imagine that everyone was moping around today. But no, not a word about their loss. They're so disenchanted."

Actually, the accountant had never seen the office manager so shut up in himself. It seemed to the accountant that, as complicated a machine as this world was, this world was not just any machine but a desperation machine if not an existence machine. Everyone was always participating in the lottery of existence.

"Real losers," the accountant said to her husband, the barber, who nodded his enormous head in his habitual obsequious gesture as if to say, *Yes, yes everyone is an idiot, but not us, so can we just sit down for a little peace, then?*

They finished eating the meals they had prepared for themselves and then poured another glass of wine and cracked open another beer. All that remained at the closing of another day were the crumbs on a stained tablecloth no one bothered to shake out. They had no lives to look forward to but the lives of their children, children who had flown the coop. Leaving them with the vacancy of unmet emotional needs.

If the accountant wasn't doing this, if she wasn't in an atmosphere of comforting and sober luxury with her husband, the barber, after a long work day, then she wouldn't have temporary leave of her anxiety—of the fierce *tom-tom* of those heart palpitations that gripped her chest and were ever more pressing, more intense, more insistent. As it was, the sense of emptiness that constituted her very being at home—that is, the one place where she didn't have to feel—the sense of calm, perfectly relaxed emptiness she was used to, once again set in.

The false light of the old, large-screen TV was now on, the fingers of the barber tightly gripping the remote control. He lay fast asleep while the accountant stared straight ahead in the pulsing blue light. The images of some docuseries were alive like a circus. She stared straight ahead and hardly blinked, as if she were still driving around that ring road, a ring road that had been drastically reduced in size and was now only as big as a traffic circle. Never going in a straight line, she circled around and around the tiny, shrunken objects at its dusty centre.

Shadow Population

"I am an enumerator, and I have never miscounted," the enumerator said aloud to himself. "I do enumeration." Driving to the Athabasca oil sands, he peered through his windshield at the sparse structures along the highway: pubs, apartment blocks, farmhouses, shops, tin-roofed buildings, roadside memorials.

Fort McMurray is a population centre—technically, an urban service area, a type of hamlet that isn't officially defined—in the Regional Municipality of Wood Buffalo, the enumerator thought. *Highway 63 is the only highway between Fort McMurray and Edmonton, and it ends, ends completely, in a dirt road just north of Fort McKay.*

The four hundred and forty-three-kilometre north-south thoroughfare to Fort McMurray and beyond went by many names: Suicide 63, Highway of Death, Hell's Highway. Semi-trucks with truly beastly loads easily made the four-hour journey an eight-hour one. And one with no rest stops. *Because*, the enumerator thought, *Fort McMurray is located in the middle of the Athabasca oil sands, where the largest and heaviest-loaded trucks carry the highest tonnage per kilometre in Canada.*

There had been no passenger rail since Canadian National discontinued the mixed train to Fort McMurray in 1989. *Just Highway 63, with its highest tonnage per kilometre in Canada.* There was a small provincial airport, but the present weather conditions didn't permit travel to it, and so there was only the highway and those who drove it.

"I am a census enumerator, and I have never lost confidential documents," he said. "I don't need to do re-enumeration because I've never left sensitive files on a subway, never sent them to the wrong house, never had my vehicle, with boxes containing hundreds and hundreds of filled-out census surveys stored away in the trunk, stolen."

The people originally in the Fort McMurray area were Cree. Cree people who knew about the Athabasca oil sands and used the surface deposits to waterproof their canoes. The area became an important junction on the fur-trade route between Eastern Canada and Athabasca Country, and so Fort McMurray was established there as a Hudson's Bay Company post in 1870, named for Chief Factor William McMurray.

"I am a census-taker, and although coverage error is at its highest rate in Alberta, there are no errors in the pages of my census." The indexers had difficulty interpreting the handwriting of other census enumerators—enumerators who entered responses incorrectly, with poor legibility, omissions, and errors; enumerators who allowed the database to contain unreliable information.

Oil exploration was happening in the early twentieth century, but the population of Fort McMurray was only a few hundred people then, the enumerator thought, having thoroughly reviewed the historical census data of his enumeration districts, preserved by the archives.

By 1921, there was serious interest in developing a refining plant to separate the oil from the sands. Fort McMurray's processing output gradually grew to over eleven hundred barrels per day by World War II. Fort McMurray and the community of Waterways amalgamated as the village of McMurray (the "Fort" was dropped until 1962, when it was restored to reflect its heritage—not the heritage of the Cree people, who knew about the Athabasca oil sands and used the surface deposits to waterproof their canoes, but rather the heritage of Factor William McMurray, who knew only that the area was an important junction on the fur-trade route) by 1947, and became a town a year later.

Fort McMurray was granted the status of new town so it could get more provincial funding. In 1967, the Great Canadian Oil Sands (now Suncor and then Syncrude) plant opened and Fort McMurray's growth soon took off. The population of the town reached six thousand eight hundred and forty-seven by 1971 and climbed to thirty-one thousand by 1981, a year after its incorporation as a city.

"I am a federal enumerator, and I am responsible for establishing an accurate and current list of eligible voters." Enumeration had all but vanished, and, having no partner beside him, the enumerator looked into the rearview mirror to affirm that he had not vanished.

"I have not vanished."

The population peaked at almost thirty-seven thousand in 1985, then declined to under thirty-four thousand by 1989. Low oil prices since the oil price collapse in 1986 slowed the oil sands production greatly. Oil price increases since 2003 made oil extraction profitable again for around a decade, until another slump in oil prices which began in December 2014 and deepened in 2015 resulted in layoffs and postponement of projects.

Layoffs that didn't worry the enumerator one bit because the Canadian government wouldn't lay off their own unless they absolutely had to. There was no bruise after the economic blow, for the public sector operated under rules that were different from those of the private sector. The rules of the public sector had improved and changed the enumerator: no longer was he so shameless, so defiant, so arrogant, mocking, and carefree. In letting himself be simply content, he had embraced his smallness. There had been a dropping off of many of his former difficulties. And he had turned much of his wishing into work. He only had to enter, make formal greetings, shake hands, speak, deal with imaginary business matters or tasks (in truth, there was no lack of other matters on his desk—a desk whose contents overflowed onto shelves), carry out orders, fetch this or that thingamajig, serve people coming and going; and then suddenly he was at a table and dining in a metropolitan manner and being waited on. As long as he was quick to obey, he was incapable of brutal and thoughtless betrayal.

On April 1, 1995, the City of Fort McMurray and Improvement District No. 143, the latter having had a population of zero, were amalgamated to form the Municipality of Wood Buffalo, which under Treaty 8 reflected the heritage and traditional lands of the Cree people, who knew about the Athabasca oil sands and used the surface deposits to waterproof their canoes. The new municipality was subsequently renamed the Regional Municipality of Wood Buffalo on August fourteenth, 1996. As a result, Fort McMurray was no longer officially designated a city. Instead, it was designated an urban service area within a specialized municipality. The amalgamation resulted in the entire RM of Wood Buffalo being under a single government.

There were no intersections. No red lights at which the enumerator had to stop. No chances to come to a complete stop, to just not be driving, to pause, to perhaps even become impatient about the small amount of time wasted—seconds, maybe minutes. To wait for the red light to turn from red to green and be happy to be driving again. No, there were absolutely no red lights. Not even a flashing red light. Because there were no intersections. Not one. He despaired and felt sad. He was so miserably small.

The RM's municipal office had been located in Fort McMurray until the May 2016 wildfire, which happened exactly ten days before Canada's seventh quinquennial official census day. It was among the one-fifth of buildings reported to be destroyed in the fire. "Record-breaking temperatures"—reaching thirty-two-point-eight degrees Celsius—and "low relative humidity" and "strong winds" contributed to the fire's rapid growth in the boreal forests surrounding the area in Northern Alberta, which had been affected by "an unusually dry and warm winter," resulting in the mandatory evacuation of more than one hundred thousand people in the city and surrounding region.

This municipal office, which was destroyed by Canada's largest recorded wildfire in history, had recorded that Fort McMurray's permanent population in 2016 was sixty-four thousand and four hundred forty-four, as counted by the RM of Wood Buffalo's 2016 municipal census. Though, even before this, the municipal census population hadn't been accepted. In other words, it hadn't been recognized for consecutive years as an official population by Alberta Municipal Affairs due to the use of statistical extrapolation by the RM of Wood Buffalo instead of one hundred percent door-to-door enumeration.

The same year, however, the RM of Wood Buffalo counted a population in its municipal census, which included a shadow population living in hotel/motel and campground accommodations, that differed from the population counted in the 2016 Canadian Census. The discrepancy in the results was attributed to differences in census methodologies: Statistics Canada used a de jure *method while the municipality used a* de facto *method.*

It was this combination that caused such a crisis for those employed by Statistics Canada: the combination of the municipal office being destroyed by Canada's largest recorded wildfire in history and the discrepancy between the census methodologies of Statistics Canada and the municipality—more accurately, the difference between the former's use of the *de jure* method (which describes practices that are "legally recognized," regardless of whether the practice "exists in reality") and the latter's use of the *de facto* method (which describes situations that "exist in reality," even if not "legally recognized").

These discrepancies in multiple realities, namely the difference between "in law" and "in fact," or "in theory" and "in practice," are what had brought the enumerator here.

He was one of twenty-five thousand enumerators, and, as such, he possessed certain expertise that allowed him to distinguish between the *de jure* method and the *de facto* method. It was because of this expertise that he was now driving Highway 63 (sometimes called Suicide 63, Highway of Death, or Hell's Highway) in a rental car—a Beamer without winter tires, the only car available at the lot—surrounded by the largest and heaviest-loaded trucks carrying the highest tonnage per kilometre in Canada. Only hours before, the enumerator had flown in from the Main Statistics Canada Building, *a four-storey federal government office building located in the Tunney's Pasture area of Ottawa, Ontario, Canada.*

He had taken the job as enumerator because it was the only way the Canadian government would forgive him his student debt—that is, as a government worker, he would eventually become debt-free. Now, he wouldn't have to worry about financing it through a bank; he wouldn't have to deal directly with those bankers who promised it would take him only half his remaining working years to recover from his debt.

The enumerator had driven along the streets of Edmonton toward the outskirts, where the housing estates disappeared and only ever-larger buildings could be seen, though they were mostly concealed by enormous fencing. *All to work out the discrepancies that have built up since the last federal census, in 2016,* he thought. It was now 2020, four years since Canada's largest recorded wildfire in history destroyed the only municipal office in Fort McMurray. And because Fort McMurray was "particularly costly to serve," StatsCan had decided to send only one of their enumerators to clear up the problem. The National Archives' Census Records were a mess in regards to this urban service area, this RM of Wood Buffalo.

"There is a risk," they had told him at the federal government office building, located in the Tunney's Pasture area of Ottawa, "of damage to our reputation," and other possible risks precisely related to "the perception that Statistics Canada does not protect respondent data, and the possibility of not obtaining this information again from these respondents."

The enumerator watched the road in front of him, which was lined with either white spruce or white birch trees. He didn't know trees. Maybe they were trembling aspen or balsam poplar. And he looked at the buildings, appearing infrequently now along the road. Trucks were sparsely scattered along its edges—not at rest stops, where you could recover from a four-hour drive that immediately became eight hours if you fell behind one of these trucks with their beastly loads, which the enumerator had done. The people behind him were trying to pass, risking their lives just to get ahead of him.

He gazed ahead, his hands on the steering wheel of the rental car—the Beamer that didn't have winter tires because nobody wanted to drive a Beamer in the Canadian winter. And in this moment, he didn't want to explain to himself again why he had insisted on approaching this menace, this city that wasn't really a city but an urban service area. Because he knew that there would be no way of ratifying the discrepancies now, no way of performing his duty. That is, counting what would amount to only a shadow population.

The workers have no idea what's going on, he thought. *These oil and gas companies tell them whatever they want*. Resulting in an inner structure built upon the logic of buddies and friends. *Buddies and friends*, he thought. *So it's impossible to know who's going, who's staying, and how much time has passed between the going and staying. There isn't a shadow of a difference for anyone in that city between working or living.*

On the plane, two business-suit guys had sat in front of the enumerator. "China only ever acquired failed oil-sands investments in the form of companies and refineries," said one to the other. "But now they own the Keystone Pipeline. The technical problems that we've been having with the pipeline—the pipeline that was supposed to pump refined petroleum to the world, just like the oil pipeline Mussolini had planned to build near Savona, Ferrania—incapable, as we were, of making a decision, that is to say a unanimous decision, on it for years, which China found extremely difficult to bear, have, in a very, very short time, that is this triptyched alliance of petrocultures—Alberta, Canada, and China—have all come to a swift conclusion—"

"But who arranged the purchase?" the other business-suit guy interrupted. "And, well, what's our position?"

"We don't know. It might just be a case of empty rumours and institutional excitements. Because about eighty percent of the world's oil reserves are state-owned. Only twenty percent are open to private investment, almost fifty percent of which are located in the Alberta oil sands. China, in the same way that it bought the Mediterranean by purchasing all of its ports, now owns the pipeline, so it's driven the major Canadian energy companies out with its transport fees alone. And then there was the economic collapse, so now there's only China, and they've also taken over traffic and transport systems, building wider expressways, twinned expressways, in all directions. It won't be just Highway 63 anymore. In fact, Albertans are voting to separate altogether from Canada, for tax exemption. For a handful of greasy paper. You know what I say. I say: hide it and forget it. My god, I myself am so forgetful of markets at the end of this era of freedoms."

The enumerator listened, glumly, bituminous, unable to follow, as the two suits talked, opined tacitly, and laughed in rotation, leaning farther down, down, and down, in the seats in front of him. So much so that he was beginning to feel confined by their chattering.

The suit continued. "Word has it that all these true-blue rawboned labourers who've been working, underqualified, for unstable six-figure incomes are now claiming their social welfare, frightened as never before, like rabbits, terribly frightened. Yes, they are rabbits, and have every reason to run like rabbits, getting out precisely as China is getting in, because they really would be in trouble otherwise, made grim and greedy by this evil black gold: oil. And so it's a state of complete abandon up there right now. People are leaving but no one is staying because they can't afford to stay and neither can they afford to leave because, well, where would they get six-figure incomes? Not from China. Never from

China. They'd be lucky to get two figures from China. Better a finger crossed than a finger burned."

It was impossible for the enumerator to understand what the suits in front of him were talking about. The entire story was just a cloud of obscurity. So he tuned out. The words reached him but he just heard them; he no longer bothered with their meaning.

And the suits spoke and spoke. They just kept talking and talking. That's what the enumerator was thinking about up there in the atmosphere—*these business-suit guys do nothing but talk and talk.* He'd been thinking about the suits even while exiting the plane. Thinking he really knew what was meant by some of these stammerings.

But what does that matter now, he thought, driving past factory buildings and tenements and fields. Here he was in the rental car, the Beamer, gliding along a concrete bridge over the Athabasca River, past the empty factory buildings and empty tenements and empty fields of the urban service centre that had once been called Fort McMurray but was now the Municipality of Wood Buffalo.

*

The enumerator stared through his windshield out into the night but saw only the empty apartment blocks of housing complexes built for workers. Then, through a gap between the buildings, a small section of the Athabasca. He had no idea what district of the city he was in.

He was hungry after what should have been a four-hour but was inevitably—*inevitably* was the right word, for how could it have been otherwise—an eight-hour drive with no rest stop, so he pulled into a Chinese restaurant called Mr. Guo's Café.

Drug dealers leaned against the café's wall, waiting for something, their dark shadows standing out clearly against the facade's filthy walls. They argued in Mandarin, their eyes like stars staring through great plumes of vaporized smoke.

Inside, everyone was Chinese except for one obese figure, who spoke in Mandarin but had trouble making the others out when they abruptly switched to their regional dialect. He sketched out gestures of hunger while saying *doii* or *doji* in a thick voice, to which people came running, while speaking in vivid accents, to give him something to eat.

He had a mask of fat, almost an inch thick, which concealed the movements of his facial muscles almost as effectively as other people's bodies hid their thoughts. Beneath that cover he could laugh or pull faces and no one would be any the wiser.

At the front of the restaurant, sitting on wicker chairs with their backs to the entrance, children peered up at a mini TV, which played rapid, jerky, silent Chinese cartoons. The oldest of the children, after watching for a long time, as though keeping track of the images on the screen required all his attention, turned to their guest, the enumerator, and said—"Shoooooort time, shoooooort time"—shortly after which the child disappeared into the back area behind the bar and never returned.

There was more than one table vacant, as everyone seemed to be crowding the bar. A gathering had formed around the elephantine man, who tried to speak in Mandarin, as did the folds of jowls under his chin, but who couldn't understand when the others spoke in their regional tongue. It was as if on purpose and without warning they would speak in their regional tongue. And then, immediately after the many-regioned voices spoke, they said something in English, which was immediately taken up as their common language.

There was something incomprehensible about this disproportionate figure, who was, in terms of height and body weight, gigantic. Frightfully obese. Immovable and impassive. Who concisely but firmly, even loudly, stated things in English and Mandarin. The elephantine man was of an uncertain age. He had great big ears and elongated lobes, and thick snow-white hair that hung in a pigtail held together by a dried-out elastic band as thick as a finger. Outsized, bulky, black-rimmed glasses sat on the bridge of his nose. The permanently-lit remainder of a cigar smoked between his sausage fingers.

The door creaked behind the enumerator. A draft blew through the room. The unexpected gust swept the restaurant cold as a group of adolescents, who it seemed had finished their transaction of drugs for money, shoved their way through. At the adolescents' table were several females of the same age, and on the table was a bottle of Hennessy XO, though no one touched it. It was there on the table, implying that they could afford it, but they didn't drink from it. Not once in the entire interval that the enumerator was standing there at the entrance did a single drop trickle down the clear bottle's neck and down anyone else's.

Then the enumerator became aware of something: a young man's singsong voice, softly droning. The older men, perhaps the owners of the restaurant, were insistent that the young man keep singing, though their chorus of encouragement was somewhat tinged, it seemed to the enumerator, with the general air of skepticism—that general air of skepticism that so characterized the adolescents, their undrunk Hennessy XO, and their forever rolling eyes. But, at the insistence of his elders, his boss, his guest, and likely himself, the young man indeed went on, didn't stop but went on, on, and on, and sang the way the older men had when they were young—that is, romantically and with emotion.

The obese figure turned his head slightly to the left and then turned the rest of his enormous body, first his thick arms and then his thick thighs. With a bloated-looking face, smiling crazily, he looked up at the young man who was singing. His enormous jowl-creases quivered like jelly.

The preamble to a business proposal, the enumerator thought, and then listened to this singing, or rather let himself hear it. And as he let himself hear it, he had the feeling that the voice wasn't so much trying to say something to him as to lull him, rock him with the musical sound of Mandarin dialect, smooth away everything inside him that was rough, everything that might spill out, everything that was aching.

The sound cautiously unfolded, and it felt good, and this was precisely what the enumerator needed. The young man continued to sing, and as he sang, the words practically fell from his mouth, as though his throat were some Northern-Chinese musical instrument, fell from his mouth in that Mandarin dialect, in a singsong drone. But it was more than just singsong and droning. It was aiming to persuade, continuously and melodiously seductive. It promised something: promised immobility, permanence, and the absence of change; promised something that vanishes at the fulfillment of that promise, and so loses the thing promised.

It promised hope but had only more hopelessness to give, and that's exactly where the enumerator was now. At the end of hope.

Retreat After Retreat

The forgotten forget nothing. They only keep on with their retreat. With measured fury, Dyson Kornfeld would go away from here. He would leave this place and set out, take off, to see the reclaimed land for himself.

To be a walking nobody.

The safety meeting wasn't safe. The protective helmet wasn't safe. The polarized goggles, the respirator mask covering his mouth, the open-face ski mask—none of it was safe. And so he stood there at the morning safety meeting, with his helmet, goggles, respirator mask, and ski mask, already waiting for the day to be done.

After the safety meeting, he looked on without a thought in his head, as did the others, who were mostly strangers. For what was there to think about while looking at the giant machine? It was enough just to be in a permanent state of fatigue, just to be not thinking, only looking at the giant machine working in the sifting tar sands.

Whenever another pipe had to be connected to the drill string, Dyson Kornfeld kept an eye on the motors, the gens, and the pumps and headed up to the drill floor. There was currently a problem down the hole, which meant he might have to "trip"—pull all the pipe out of the hole and fix the problem. A drill bit might need to be changed, or he might need to adjust the setting on the tool that steered the drill bit. Tripping took a lot out of him. Extreme physical exertion followed by brief periods of rest, over and over, again and again, until all the pipe was out of the hole and the problem could be fixed. Then it was the same thing in reverse order, until the bit was back on the bottom and the driller could drill again.

The weather, the work, and the people were all depressingly common to Dyson Kornfeld. There had been several accidents in recent months. The company's ownership had changed hands, and many of the new heavy-machine operators drank on the job. These new crewmates, moving from rig to rig, accepting less and less pay for more and more risk, were quickly earning a reputation of drinking on the job. Dyson Kornfeld had managed to stay rep-free all these years because he avoided the three cardinal sins on the oil rig: don't drop anything down a hole, don't harm others, and don't get hurt. Until the increase in accidents, these rules had seemed stupidly obvious to him. How was it possible that in a militant environment such as this, where everything was supervised a thousand times over, a drunk was able to operate heavy machinery?

Dyson Kornfeld viewed each individual as a direct insult. No one wanted to be there anymore, but they did want to remain in what was familiar. No one wanted to make an irreversible decision. Because the misery, the depravity, and the many rough deeds would forge them into something like a mass of iron. Grimly, they stared ahead. Grim, dull, unconscious anger, united them.

Needing to trip after all, he trundled the pipe a little further along. He adjusted his gloves, grabbed the pipe, staggered back until it was completely out of the hole, and then pushed it out and over to where the other crew members stood ready to take it from him.

Dyson Kornfeld had been doing this for nearly five years, with annual raises in pay. The company paid six figures for a derrickhand, more if you had your own accommodations outside the camp. Six figures. Not salary, like the brass, but hourly: thirty-seven dollars an /hour (one hundred and forty dollars if you had your own accommodation, as he did now), eighty-four hours a week, and a living allowance. That was how much they used to pay him as a derrickhand. He perspired in the winter sun, the suffocating tar sands. When working overtime, he saw the Alberta sunset, the industrial night, and sometimes the northern lights.

Fourteen days on followed by two days off. Eight months away at work and four months at home.

It's time for a break, Dyson Kornfeld thought. *Time for a break.*

"You'll never get paid six figures again, don't even dream about it," the new overseer at the tar sands had told Dyson Kornfeld. Since the company had been bought out, he'd had no choice but to accept a reduction in his pay and hope he wouldn't be let go. "Be glad you ever got six figures, like the others." All his crewmates had been dulled by a decrease in salary. All of them were becoming as useless as carts with no wheels.

The other crew wouldn't show up for their safety meeting until six-thirty P.M., at the cross-shift. After a brief rundown of whatever Dyson Kornfeld's crew had been working on, the new crew would pick up where they left off. At seven thirty, Dyson Kornfeld's crew would finally pile into the truck and head off.

On endless repeat.

Dyson Kornfeld left the line early and headed for the mine's exit. No one called out after him. Perhaps no one even noticed. The city lay to the left. He had to keep away from houses. Meeting someone would instantly mess up the whole thing. Taking quick steps past the lower edge of the city, he soon found what he was looking for.

He was looking for Highway 63. It ran from Fort McMurray through the boreal forest to Edmonton. But he wasn't trying to get to Edmonton. He just needed to get to his backpack.

He set out on the sparkling, crunching snow toward his empty hotel room. The ground was practically steaming in the cold—even through the thick soles of his boots he could feel it. He clapped his hands together to warm them, took a deep gulp of air, and was seized by a violent coughing fit. He breathed through his nostrils, inhaling the acrid smell of his perspiration.

A cousin had once told him that he'd have to sell his soul to make money at the oil field, that it would turn his soul the colour of oil. And sometimes, it seemed as though his cousin had been right. Throughout his childhood, seemingly the whole community of Cold Lake had said, "This oil has to be appreciated. It's ten percent of the world's oil reserves—almost two trillion barrels—but only a hundred billion are recoverable, which is to say it won't last forever." He'd never understood what they meant.

When he was first hired as a derrickhand, Dyson Kornfeld was so intimidated by everything that he was supposed to learn all at once, and he had to muster so much strength in order not to collapse every hour from exhaustion, that it never occurred to him to pause in front of the oil just to see for himself what made it the most important oil in the world. And, anyway, the supervisor was watching him every moment. Dyson Kornfeld wouldn't have dared to take a single step without the man's authorization. Crude oil became for him just another black liquid—a black liquid he had to struggle with again and again, day after day. And now, the new overseer's eyes were always on him.

I have no soul. No one here does. Dyson Kornfeld was therefore the man who'd sold his shadow, making him the shadow of the man who'd sold it. *And there's really nothing else you can do. You can't work in the tar sands until you grow old.* Not now. Not since a hundred thousand pink slips had been sent out.

He would live out his days in wretched drunkenness. A great shadow had been cast over everyone like him, and in this great shadow, his family life would fall to ruin. For, if he was no longer making six figures, how could his family life not fall to ruin? Dyson Kornfeld knew that he would never go back. He knew there was no place for him there, or anywhere in the world. He would go away now, no matter what happened. He would set out and go north and see the reclaimed land.

His feet were burning with fatigue, his waist and back hurt, his neck hurt, his shoulders hurt, his head was about to fall off, and something was stinging in his eyes. How long had he been walking? Dyson Kornfeld wouldn't sit down because he knew he wouldn't be able to get up again. He trudged on with haste, mindlessly and desperately. It was difficult to tell which was scarier.

It would have been untrue to claim that he didn't know what crude oil was like, but had someone asked him, Dyson Kornfeld would have said, "It's black." He could see it in his mind, as if he were next to the scandalous, frothing scum of a surface deposit. He could see it: thick, leaden, sticky, filthy. Below the surface, light gradually withdrew from the world. The deposit became like blood. Millennia later, the oil would gush again from these sands. *Like blood*, he thought. Like dark blood. Laughing blood. *I was already living today from that oil that will gush in millennia*, Dyson Kornfeld thought, *because in this millennium, I am already that oil.*

Back in his hotel room, Dyson Kornfeld stood behind the thick curtain looking down at the whirling commotion on the street. For the first time, he was truly panicking. The panic screamed like sirens in his head. He leaned one shoulder against the wall, casting an occasional glance at the grimy bed, at his backpack. He had to think of his backpack. It had to be packed and ready to go, and so he started doing that. First, he collected his toiletries from the bathroom and tossed them in the backpack, not bothering to organize them. Same with the T-shirts, the library book on land reclamation in Canada, the change of long johns, the safety manual, the phone, the compass, the rain jacket, the medicine box, the wallet, and the map, one after another. And when everything was in the backpack, and he'd pulled the last zipper closed, Dyson Kornfeld looked up at the ceiling, at the plaster peeling in layers.

At one hundred mg, secobarbital sodium treated insomnia and anxiety. At two hundred mg, it could be used for preoperative sedation. Picking apart capsule after capsule, Dyson Kornfeld mixed nine thousand mg, a euthanasia drug, into a plastic bottle of whisky-sweetened water and put it in the bottle holder of his backpack.

Using the utmost caution, Dyson Kornfeld slipped out the door, not wanting to be seen by his crewmates, who would probably be returning from the mine soon, tiptoed downstairs, sneaked past the reception desk of the empty hotel, stepped onto the street, and turned at the first corner.

Dyson Kornfeld sat in his truck, which was idling in the hotel's parking lot. He pulled out his map of Northern Alberta and the Northwest Territories and spread it on his knees, placing a crooked finger on Fort McMurray. From Fort McMurray, he traced a line north along the Athabasca, passing between MacDonald Island Park and Tar Island, northwest to the Peace Region, and then continued on the south bank of Peace River, east to the town of Wabasca, past the industrial zones, and onto the Athabasca oil sands, north of the fort at McKay. There, he tapped the threadbare map. His finger had traveled so often from Fort McMurray to the reclamation sites that the blue line of the Athabasca had worn away.

The more than thirty kilometres ahead of him, because traffic was annoyingly slow, threatened to be unbearably tedious, weary as he was of the desolation rippling past his window: flatland, snow, trees, hamlet. It was thirty kilometres north of Fort McMurray that he was going.

The signs at the trailhead were in Cree: *Matcheetawin* ("the beginning place") and *Sagow Pematosowin* ("living in peaceful coexistence with the land"). The four-kilometre interpretive-trail system wound through various types of reclaimed land: four thousand and sixty-nine hectares of reclaimed land. Fifty hectares of spruce, aspen, and jack-pine forests, grasslands, wetlands, nineteen hectares of bird-watching areas, and a herd of three hundred miserable wood bison on four thousand miserable hectares, all of which comprised the former tailing ponds of the oil-sands operations. *That's fifty plus nineteen plus four thousand, which makes four thousand and sixty-nine hectares of reclaimed land, of municipal woods. Measured,* he thought, *in the volume of material then, before the human disturbance, and the volume of material now, after the disturbance.*

The *swish-swash* of his holstered water bottle was becoming a powerless horror compared to the articulated alienation he felt in this last place, in the horrid purple of his life. He would not reverse climate change by snuffing out his own existence, but he would at least become a good ground zero. He could say no to the recuperative habits of human beings, who always saw the world as theirs.

Dyson Kornfeld was a little late reaching his destination, a remote spot in the middle of the forest, deep in the overgrown industrial zone, now a realm of pines, firs, and spruces. And as time wore on, he felt a growing fear that some wolf was awaiting him there. An impenetrable wall of greenery blocked out everything but the path. It rose before his eyes like a cliff face. He was at what appeared to be a dark expanse of marshland at the heart of the reclaimed forest.

The fateful purple hour had come, and so he took careful hold of the water bottle and sipped the nine thousand mg of secobarbital sodium. Sickly sweet and yet still bitter, not just as he would have liked it. His hands shook, he couldn't keep his lips shaped to the rim of the bottle, and the liquid dribbled out of the corners of his mouth. It began to go to his head. He stopped himself. Took a breath. Swallowed and continued, until it looked as if there was only a drop left in the shoulder of the bottle.

The brownish light of the liquid that had been inside the water bottle now seemed to surround him. He stood there for a long time, for there was something, something that he couldn't quite understand. It felt as if he hadn't yet been born. It was as if he was swimming in some element before birth.

That volume of material living in the horror of the human disturbance had come and gone, had been traded in for a before-and-after effect, traded in for the mysterious effects these restoration sites had on tourists. The province issued reclamation certificates to encourage remediation, not at all to discourage mining or drilling. The largest energy companies only needed to make it seem as if the death had been happy—the death of what had previously existed on these four thousand and sixty-nine hectares of reclaimed land, of municipal woods; four thousand and sixty-nine hectares of reclaimed land being the approximate volume of material then, before the human disturbance, and the approximate volume of material now, after the disturbance. But what about that volume of anonymous material before the disturbance? And the horrific fascination—obsession—humans had with its reduction into a black matter of oblivion, thick and opaque? Not so long ago, it had been a living material living in its own nonhuman time. Nonhuman material living in flower-seconds, tree-minutes, forest-hours, mountain-days, planet-years, solar-centuries, cosmic-millennia.

A breeze. The fidgeting of branches. A loon hooting.

Dyson Kornfeld imagined bodies of that anonymous material emerging out of mud, bodies between origin and death, embodiment and dissolution, composition and decomposition, and the convulsions in the convergence of these two points. Because a millennium later, the secret oil would gush again from these sands. *Like a desire or a deadly infection,* Dyson Kornfeld thought. *An infection that spreads like a rotten black sun, an incomprehensible sun that rots as it rises from the black, meat-like decay of the earth. Yes, a kind of black sun of the crisis of the West, rising up and up, into those dreadful heights of desire, rotting our souls as it rises.*

I was already living today from that oil that will gush in millennia, because in this millennium, I am already that oil.

Dyson Kornfeld felt somewhat idiotic for having thought about it in such an abstract way.

Rustling. Silence. Footsteps on gravel. Silence.

He knew exactly what products were derived from a barrel of heavy, sour feedstock—mostly gasoline, then of course diesel and jet fuel, heavy fuel and light fuel, and also propane or butane or some other consumer product, asphalt being produced the least. How could he not know this? For they had been giving Dyson Kornfeld nothing but this, this information on the oil sands, to read, and for five years he'd read nothing but what they'd given him to read.

Dyson Kornfeld recognized the overall process. Three basic steps: extraction, upgrading, and refining. Each step of the process needed bigger and bigger factories. *Bit-u-men.* He emphasized the weight in each syllable. *Nothing but sand and water. Just eighty-five percent sand and just five percent water, the ten percent residual being almost anything and so nothing useful. No more than a pumpable slurry, until it's recovered.*

The whole process was moving from shallow deposits to deep deposits. And Dyson Kornfeld and his crewmates were absent in this new scenario. They were an optional, intermediary step. Whether an old or new technique was used depended on the depth of the deposit. The operation could either mine the whole deposit and let gravity separate the bit-u-men or extract the bit-u-men in place (in situ) using steam, without disturbing the land. But they always placed the onus on the end user. As the brass put it: "About eighty percent of the GHGs contained in a barrel of oil [of which they produced several million per day, a hundred billion per year] are emitted by the end user during combustion."

In symbolizing the Earth, we have already left the Earth behind, Dyson Kornfeld thought. These reclamation areas, in symbolizing the Earth, were not the Earth. It was customary to not speak of the death of animals if they could avoid it, but these creatures were what made the crude oil such a terribly complex hydrocarbon. *Because the Earth's biomass is stable. Everything that falls and dies becomes nourishment for that which comes after.*

There was something so utterly poor about the quality of the restoration sites. And as high-profile an operation as the reclamation was, involving expert environmentalists and tree planters, it seemed to Dyson Kornfeld to be a very mixed success. In a book from the district's small library, he'd seen pictures of what the area had been like before. There was an ugliness now, an ugliness, yes. *Very ugly.* A deeply symbolic attachment, the last meaningful connection, the one people claimed to have with nature, was absent.

And as Dyson Kornfeld followed the system of trails named after Cree words, one meaning "the beginning place" and the other "living in peaceful coexistence with the land," he wondered what new beginning there could be. When and where had this new beginning started? And what exactly was peacefully coexisting with the land here? *Us—the Cree, the tourists, foreign investors, scientists, politicians, rig workers, me—or them, whoever they are— the restored whatchamacallits of the area?* It all seemed to be evidence of a sophisticated cruelty.

Dyson Kornfeld placed himself in the secluded beauty of the restoration site and felt, in a tangled way, that the green of the trees was already part of his blood. *The only way to experience new sensations is to build yourself a soul,* he thought. That was, after all, what the monsters of forward progress were so frantically obsessed with accomplishing. They wanted to construct something like a new soul, to unbody the old one and ensoul the new body. *Because things are the way we feel them to be and people feel nothing for nature that is not human nature. And the only way to have new things is to feel in a different way. And the only way to feel new things is to find a new way of feeling them.*

Retreating, to be a walking nobody on this lone and lonely walk, Dyson Kornfeld thought. *Retreating, to be a dead walker in these snowy municipal woods. Retreating, to be an eerie photograph of a dead man in the snow. And to return, he thought, in a millennium, as oil. Because in this millennium I am already that oil of the next millennium, and for the dead, a single day must be as a thousand years and a thousand years but a single day. And so centuries pass.*

Life was retreating.

Before he could succeed in blacking out, Dyson Kornfeld put his finger in his mouth. He could remember, no, he could feel himself grabbing hold of his thick wet tongue and lifting it up in search of the pharyngeal reflex. The hairy knuckles of his thick fingers rubbed against his palate; a broad nail bumped against his uvula. He jabbed his gullet. Gagged, then vomited. Left behind was a bitter taste of secobarbital sodium and whisky.

The Naysayer

THE DESTRUCTIVE WORK: First Phase

The Inner Lie

(*first version*)

The Last Refuge of Hope. The sensation of living was always painful for me. So I quickly excluded myself from life's aims and directions. I thought that ending all contact with everything would be the best thing. Finding ways to avoid action would then be my only necessary action. Although, I still breathed. I still moved. These were the hard facts regarding the human condition. I decided I had to either detest action, for which I was born, or detest the dream, for which no one was ever born. But since I detested both equally, I chose neither and mixed one thing with the other, and it was like mixing two nauseating spirits. I became drunk on error and erroneously alive.

I feel. I am free and lost.

I can tell only the first part of a much longer story. And it will be told in the horrific quantity of beginnings that I would have written down, had it been possible to. But it wasn't possible, because everything is a beginning and nothing ever happens without one. So it's from one false start to another false start that I begin this story, so to speak, as it strives toward a future that can never occur. It's like a grueling trip from point A to point B with the distance between points always increasing. And so I go slowly, guessing at where those two points should be.

And in precisely this way, I am a person who never existed, who never will exist. What no longer exists in me strives toward what doesn't yet exist, what will never exist again.

I chose the wrong means of escape. I took an awkward shortcut that led me right back to where I was, left to compound the horror of living there, in that place of no escape, with the exhaustion of the journey. Empty-handed and up to my ears in student debt. If I wasn't a destroyed human being then, I am now. Stagnant and useless. Full of false sensation. False scorn and feeble hatred. Not knowing which it really is, scorn or hatred, I laugh.

Because my feelings are a confused yet lucid mistake. Life, despite all its griefs and fears and jolts, should be happy. And yet, for me, life has never stopped hurting. I've never stopped hurting. I'm always sad, however happy or content I may often feel. And the part of me that realizes this stands a little behind me. I am just a face in the window panes of this house.

For me, life is just a bridge between two mysteries. *A bridge with no idea how it was built,* I think, and I immediately don't understand what I'm saying. Because what I meant to say was, "A bridge with no idea how I was built," and that makes even less sense than the metaphor, so I'll move on.

I closed myself off from the world. But closing myself off didn't bring me anything.

When I have fully closed myself off from the human world, I thought, *then, then and only then, I will touch the strange root of it all. My emptiness is my measure, and the great emptiness in me will be my place for existing, not the human world, since the human world is thought and only my thoughts are what make it mean anything for me, in my longing to discover the meaning of my existence. But life itself can have no meaning. Otherwise it would not be.*

I was convinced that there was no greater part of the whole worth thinking about than the part of the greater whole that was myself. That is, if the human world was only thinking, only my thoughts mattered.

If you could only know the solitude of those first steps of mine. It wasn't like the solitude of a human being. It was as if I'd already died and was taking those first steps alone into another life. I shrunk into the marrow of my cold, hypothetical bones; my last foolish refuge was a skeletal sorrow.

My destiny is just this and nothing else: to search as if to find something and then to return empty-handed. As a captive in this prison of time, I realize how the unsayable can be given to me only through the failure of my actions, which is a language. It's the language of the naysayer. An ancient language that I needed to learn.

Only when the construction fails can I obtain what it could not achieve.

Our failures stand, half-finished, as beautiful as the ruins of some stone conception. But ruins are also memorials to their creators. Persistence is our effort; giving up is the reward. One only reaches it having experienced the power of building and preferring to give up. Giving up must be a choice. Giving up is the most sacred choice of a life. Giving up is the true human instant. And this alone is the very glory of my condition.

Giving up is a revelation.

So let us make ourselves into humans, pretend ones, if only just for the duration of these beginnings, of this story, until we reach the point where we no longer know what we are, because the truth is that we are pretend humans and we really don't know what we are.

I am I.

I am nobody.

I am sick and tired of myself.

The Disquieting Questions

(*second version*)

A Theory of Giving Up. The longed-for space had been found. It was on the top floor of an enormous grey building on one of the side streets that traced crooked zigzags between Vernon and Coburg. A thirteen-inch computer screen posting an advertisement had miraculously turned into my lodgings for the next academic period.

The room was somewhat narrow and dark, but once the electric light had been switched on, I noticed the shapeless pieces of furniture around me, the design on the old wallpaper, how the shabby walls met in the shape of an A and ran in long verticals until they reached the kitchenette, and then on to a door that led into a permanently vacant spare room, at the back of the house. I immediately went to the dusty windowpane at the front of the house. Looked out over hundreds and hundreds of rooftops. Deserted streets with dead windows.

There and then, I felt the pleasurable sweetness of having neither family nor companion. The vague disquiet that comes with being far from home set in, and I was then like an unwritten page. I was galvanized.

A crease between her long, thin eyebrows, her lip trembling slightly, the co-owner of the house, Mrs. Stefan, said, "Those who have keys have rights. As the German proverb goes: 'Locks and keys are not made for honest fingers.' You have a key, but no one else must have one like it. Understood? It's important that only you have rights in this house, not your visitors. Understood?"

I told her I understood and she left me with that sensation of burning, a sensation that spread throughout my body like a fever of feeling. Alone. Finally. Alone.

I lived by myself in a room that was full of shadows. It held a bed, a table, and two chairs. The walls were bare except for a

Malocchio talisman I'd hung over the door, where a finger-length brass crucifix used to be. But the desired effect had not been produced. Instead of creating a feeling of anarchic spirituality, or an arbitrary, pervasive sense of dread in the safest and most secure of situations, the evil eye remained calm and decorative. Almost Bohemian.

Sometimes in the morning, I'd hear a flute playing on the floor below mine, where the Stefans lived. This was among my first observations of what I would soon recognize as my daily routine. When the flute played, I would picture the husband. Mrs. Stefan had told me he was an old philosopher who'd retired as a professor and founder of the program at the university—the program and the university I'd come all this way to attend. When I tried to picture this strange figure I'd never met (and never would) playing the flute, I saw him putting his hand in his housecoat, taking out his flute in three pieces, and screwing it together. Then he'd blow into that dismal Schopenhauerian device of his. He produced the most sorrowful sounds, and the tune, if there was one, was always half-remembered. Sometimes it would become inaudible, and then, as if he'd become aware of the absence, the doleful sound would return.

Most nights, rain fell on my window. Most nights, I lay half-awake. A gust of wind might make a bird beat rapid wings against the glass. A late-night cart might jostle roughly over the cement beneath the window before disappearing down the street. Now and then, a door on the stairs might slam. Sometimes there were footsteps going into the spare room. Sometimes, just silence, and the foretaste of a nightmare in my mouth.

I found myself with my back against the wall most nights. Sometimes all night. During these spells of insomnia, I usually listened to Bach: Glenn Gould's *The Goldberg Variations*. On those nights, the inanimate things over which I tried to obtain control took the field against me. When I touched something, it spilled or rolled to the floor. The collar buttons of shirts disappeared under the bed, the point of the pencil broke, the handle of the razor fell off, the window shade refused to stay down. I fought back but with too much violence and was decisively defeated, again and again, by the spring of the alarm clock.

One day, after morosely eating soft-boiled eggs in the kitchen, I reviewed the bookshelves in the spare room with a keener eye. And as I was doing so, a plump German tome slipped out of my fingers and flopped onto the floor. It had been securely bound, but then it got loose, and all I know about this is that the same thing that had unleashed it had secured it before. I had unleashed what had been securely bound and a random line in that open book caught my eye.

I sat in the lap of a leather monster, a couch swollen with padding and tense with springs, in that spare room. And I was soon to find out that the book was the most laconic, scholastic-like, and absorbing publication I'd ever read: the tome, titled *A Theory of Giving Up*, provided a "complete taxonomy of failure."

At first glance, a theory of giving up might seem intellectual, dull, devoid of imagery, stiff, and starchy: something that comprised statements, arguments, pleas, and revelations. But when read with a certain imagination, the dry, lapidary style only intensified a sense of the fantastic. It pushed one to the most surprising, unexpected conclusions. Even the notes at the back of the book were uncommon. For instance:

Oblivion: a long-in-the-making but instantaneous collapse; here and gone; to the absolute nectar of vacuity.

I entered this thought and many others like it, and I didn't suspect that I'd never come out, that I'd get stuck, as it were, inside of that immeasurably vast, baffling system that was truly immeasurable, truly baffling. Instead of constantly roaming from my consciousness to my unconsciousness and back again, I went so far into my unconsciousness that I couldn't find my way back to my consciousness. I began to wonder about my existence: How will I perish? What failure is in store for me? And I found myself running a neurotic finger, line by line, down that taxonomy of failure, as if to find my designated type.

Trying and failing. Failing to appreciate this.
Trying and trying again. Failing and failing again.
Failing better. Each time.
Not bothering to try in the first place.
Failing, unaware that one has been trying.
Failing, unaware that one has failed.
Trying awkwardly, failing awkwardly.
Bewildering failure.
Clinical failure.
Certain effort, uncertain failure.
The mind is willing, the body unable; the body is willing, the mind unable.
Failure to fail.
Successful failure. [...]

On the flyleaf was a name: Detlef Stefan.

It was the old philosopher's own work. He'd constructed a whole metaphysical system of misfortune.

I soon found his picture, the only one I would ever see of him, in one of the university's halls while roaming through the desolate corridors of academia and trying to determine what four walls would hold my attention in their doubtful aviaries.

Detlef Stefan had the face of a university lecturer: a knobby, erudite forehead; a thoughtful and strange weariness in his eyes, which sat under a corrugated brow, as if he were half-furious and half-nauseated; a whitish beard; and hair combed over a bald crown. He had, incidentally, been a lecturer on the categorical Kant and paradoxical Hegel. And I read in his compressed, old-man face that he must have donned ceremonial robes in order to write in secret.

His life was one long "standing at the window," I decided, after reading what I'd read in the tome. He had created inside himself a philosopher. A philosopher who carefully sets out his philosophies for himself, while he, gazing at his reflection in the window of his house, replaces himself with his dream. The book was a single state of soul: the mumblings of a grumbler. And this soul was analyzed from every angle, traversed in every possible direction, it seemed. In it, he held the most contradictory opinions, the most diverse beliefs, precisely because he never thought them or spoke them or acted them out to anyone. Instead: the tome.

In the first few days of sudden autumn, before summer ended and real autumn arrived, an autumn that was to be as autumn as a tomb, the Stefans were at their Lunenburg cottage. And all that monotonous month of August, I read the tome. The retired professor was in ill health, Mrs. Stefan had said to me when I was in the process of moving my furniture up to the top floor, and that he needed "as much fresh air as possible" before the cooler winter months set in.

That autumn would take everything—everything I thought and dreamed, everything I did and did not do, discarded scraps of paper, religions and philosophies that drowsy children of the abyss play at making. That autumn. Yes. That autumn would take everything that made up my soul—from my greatest aspirations to the ordinary house in which I lived to the gods I'd never worship to the bosses I'd never work for. That autumn would take everything, its painful indifference beginning in me rather than in the world. That autumn would take everything.

Resignation first began to germinate in my heart after I saw the tome. I cannot put into words what the tome's system was, exactly. Perhaps it was a philosophy of futility. Still, I lived in its deep, resounding tones. I've lived in them ever since.

I organized myself inside the hope of having become completely futile, failed, and feeble. Because if I no longer had this hope, I would also lose the marvelous hope of freeing myself one day from the dreaded taxonomy of failure. And thinking back now on the thoughts I had then, I realize that my old life was necessary to me because, without that life I led, I would not have known what my failure was.

The system in the tome, the system in which I have lived ever since, even went so far as to reduce hope to a simple result of constructing and counterfeiting without denying that something to hope for existed. As if hope had been categorically hunted out of the theory. It was like the ruins of buildings that were never more than ruins because someone, in the middle of building, grew tired of wanting to build.

I was able to describe only the smallest details of the tome, excerpts and aphorisms mostly—only fragments of what I saw. I don't know if I'm the better or worse for having wrested those pages from oblivion, but I archived all that I could into a series of alphabetized notebooks, from Notebook A through to Notebook M.

Notebook A

1 Postpone everything. Never do today what you can put off until tomorrow. You don't have to do anything, tomorrow or today. [...]

2 Never think about what you're going to do. Simply don't do it. Respect nothing and believe in nothing. Flee from all provocative material. [...] Live your life. Do not be lived by it. In truth and in error, in sickness and in health, be your own self. Dream. [...]

3 The aristocracy lies in not touching. Do not get too close. If you do, your dream will die, and the touched object will take over your feelings. Because nothing is what it is, and yet dreams are always dreams. Seeing and hearing are the only noble things life contains. [...] Be pure to be yourself.

4 Abstain internally from action, taking no interest in things, with perfect objectivity—since there is no point, no reason to change the way things already are. [...]

5 The highest stage of dreaming is reached when, having created a cast of characters, you live them all, all at the same time—you are all those souls jointly and interactively. It involves no faith, not even a god.

6 You are God. You are yourself the end and limit of your own desire.

7 In dreams you must achieve everything. How many countless things have you been, yet you were never like the real thing. It was a thing of no importance and no one died. To sleep is to fuse with God, a personal Nirvana.

8 The task of giving up will take you your whole lifetime. [...]

It all comes down to trying to experience tedium in a way that doesn't hurt, I thought. That was, at least as far as the author of the tome was concerned, the cure for human happiness. The tome was like a handbook on inertia.

From the room on the fourth floor, adjacent to the last step of the spiral staircase, I made my weekly descent to the basement to do my laundry. Among the terribly dreary prints (some of which were the Stefans' daughters' early charcoal sketches) on the cramped walls along either side of the stairs was a small rectangular frame containing a picture of what I assumed to be their property in the country: a cottage shrouded by mist.

Once in the basement, where the ceiling was so low I had to hunch uncomfortably, I loaded the washing machine and then decided to lie down on the lino-covered floor. Under the stairs, ranks of benevolent-looking jars of preserves were arranged along shelves with military precision. Here was everything Mrs. Stefan had had time to bottle since the beginning of summer: fruit in syrup and other various savouries; tomato juice; walnuts preserved in honey. I ran my eye over the glittering glassware, not quite knowing which to choose, and finally decided on a jar of boiled peaches in rum.

As I ascended the stairs, I noticed that the door to the Stefans' floor stood ajar. I knocked. No one came. I pushed the handle. The door gave. The first room contained only books. I called out. No answer. Puzzled, I peeped through an open door into the next room: a table, and drawn up to it, an armchair. I imagined what Detlef Stefan would have looked like had he been in that armchair: forehead slumped on the table, limp arms grazing the floor. There, where he wasn't, stacks of notes were everywhere, and all his books were brimming full of marginalia. *He must be so afraid of being struck down by completion*, I thought, as I swallowed an entire boiled peach. It slipped down my throat like an eel.

Several weeks later, after the Stefans had returned from their cottage, I found myself rummaging through my own paper piles. Old, useless jottings kept thrusting themselves into my hands: data, university junk, odd passages from books, unfounded hypotheses, doubts, official communications, the latest news. The one thing I needed was not there: the large plumb tome with the jumping lines hidden inside. It had disappeared. Apparently forever. A whole systematic philosophy constructed by accident, lost. I had lost a whole system.

I quickly dressed and left the house. On the street, I walked straight ahead, without turning right or left, without knowing where or why. I wept like a god who has been robbed of his newly-created universe. An undreamed-of universe. Meanwhile, the streetlights had turned an exaggeratedly slow yellow, a yellow grimed with grey, and the green of the trees was a different green, filled as much with silence as with lights and colours. Unknown lamps bloomed behind windows in the black of the night.

I must have left it out somewhere in the house, I thought. *Who knows what he'll do with it now.* He had created it expressly for his own eyes. And knowing that I'd most likely seen it, he had certainly, knowing a thing often happens more than once if it can happen at all, destroyed it. This had to have been the case, because when I returned home, the door to the Stefans' floor was again locked and there was only an empty bookshelf in the spare room where the tome had once been. The dead bookshelf was all that he'd left me to understand of his theory of giving up.

Nietzsche Is Dead! An unskilled hand had daubed the words in yellow paint on a bathroom-stall door. *God is Dead!*

God had been crossed out and replaced with *Nietzsche*; underneath was a long list of retorts and other scratched-out names. The names alone opened doors to the uncertain. All I could think of when I read this aphorism was how killing what had never been was rare, sublime, absurd.

The dead are beautiful. *But to live, to survive*, I thought, *well, to survive is to become ugly and contaminated.*

The atmosphere at the university was suffocating. Old eyes appeared. And people. They had a familiar way of looking at you: not at, but through. You couldn't hide your emptiness. They would bore into you with their pupils. *They will walk right through you, as through air. Because, to them, you have become defaced, faded, as discoloured as air.*

No new students were entering the program. I was always waiting for them to enter, and that weakened me. It seemed as if we, the students who remained, had only a little time left to breathe, sleep, wake up. We still believed in literature, still believed in the endurance of the Being of the human being.

When we lost this belief, we lost everything.

I cannot read anything now because I see only defects, imperfections, possible improvements. Philosophy has lost its therapeutic function for me. Because, like those other students, I now know that all systems are defensible and intellectually possible; and so I lack the ability to forget that the aim of all metaphysical speculation is the search for truth.

In a class on the history of the No, honest questions became dishonest replies. Boyishly ebullient chatter. Intrigue, gossip, boasting. In the warp of furtive glances, mute dissent or mute consent. More than half the class was indefinitely absent, so I reviewed my notes, silently and respectfully:

— Pyrrho of Elis: doubt doesn't stop, or doubt stops at tranquility.

— It is said that, finding himself unable to decide which philosophical school of his day to support, Pyrrho discovered a state of stillness and quiet [...]

After all this, why in the world would anyone finish writing a paper? I thought. *The professor should only pass the students who are incapable of finishing the course.* We were at an institute of broken columns and dead stone. And it was as if they were beating me with my own life. It weighed on me as if it were sentencing me not to death but to knowledge. It stole things from me, and afterwards it had no idea what to do with me. So it spread sorrow for fun.

Between classes, in the inner courtyard connecting the old and new wings, I ran, breathlessly, into what I took for a dark and ancient stain on a dense curvilinear column: a classmate. I felt the awkwardness of anatomy.

An ash glowed between her teeth.

A shy caesura.

"I wanted to be the queen on one of those old playing cards everyone has at home," Harlan said, exhaling both her words and the smoke into my face. The smoke blinded my eyes while it curled around the whites of hers. "Being a picture would be an ambition worthy of a modern woman. Don't you think?"

Harlan seemed to me as mysterious as a sad thought in a moment of joy. Then I thought: *She is the person I am when I actually know myself.*

I'd always pretended there was nothing to a person besides their head. I'd never noticed her, or really anyone, below the neck. Still, it was clear to me that my attention with Harlan was constantly split between the head and the groin. Between the two zones of modesty.

Her necklace of fake pearls accentuated the fragility of her graceful brown neck. Her floral-print blouse depicted carnations. Sad blossoms. A short, dark blue pinafore clung to her hips and bound her long thighs tightly together while indicating the lines of her triangular dream. I imagined an hour made flesh with her. Skin against skin in the darkness of a naked universe and all that unwashed sexuality. An entire unwritten book of sensations. And then my imagination felt the terrible grief of love without depth. And without depth, there was only my timidity and incompetence. Her thick, soft lips soberly celebrated the irony of their own smile as she leaned against the column.

"You've been here as long as I have, haven't you?" Harlan asked. "Studying, I mean. But I never see you with anyone. Don't you have any friends here?" She raised her gorgeous eyebrows and smiled. Her nipples pressed delicately against her blouse. Then she turned her face away and the sparkling black

Frenchness of the hair that was held in place by pomade tumbled lightly over her gentle shoulders.

My face crimsoned at my erotic afterthought.

"Friends, none," I said. "Just a few acquaintances who think they get on with me." And then my voice dried up, as if to pronounce the words out loud were a kind of embarrassment at my own existence. I didn't believe in the friendship shown me here, at this institute. I never doubted for a moment that they would all betray me, and yet I was always shocked when they did. But everyone was potentially interesting and convertible into dream material, into other people, and so I was always polite, genuinely liking them, though admittedly self-interested and indifferent to others' opinions. I noticed that sometimes I frightened these people, but what they really feared was themselves.

I felt what I had said in my thoughts to myself, and then what I had said with my unfeeling eyes to her. And then I moved on like a large, cruel cat. I pitied myself.

I thought of adding to the list on the bathroom-stall door: "I am shy with women, therefore God does not exist."

War or Reasoning. Often, the feeling of a great inner defeat came over me. In me, the inability to act was an affliction that had its origins in metaphysics. I always feared that any movement on my part would dislodge the stars or alter the sky. According to my way of experiencing things, any gesture implied a perturbation, a fragmentation, of the external world. I acquired, with regard to action, a transcendental honesty that, once I became aware of it, inhibited me from having any strong links with the tangible world. And so began the scholastic stagnation of my life.

Dr. Daniel Brandes was part of the reason for my obsession with metaphysics. Because of him I found lurking in myself a metaphysics of deep, autonomous shadows. I found my metaphysical enemy.

He was a paradox: a Jew who taught Heidegger. He taught everything, preached everything, aroused all emotions. "Because action, whether it be war or reasoning, is right, and peace, pointless without action," he would say to our class, the only class that students would attend regularly.

So, I decided I would be without action: I will teach nothing, preach nothing, arouse no emotion. Because war is everywhere that reason is.

For almost every lecture, Dr. Daniel Brandes would prepare a neat and tidy essay, which he'd read aloud to the class. An essay that evoked belief in some kind of ancient present. "Because," Dr. Daniel Brandes would say, "everything, when it did exist, existed in the present, because all things belong to the present."

The disquieting question "Where is God, even if he doesn't exist?" was to remain unanswered. Dr. Daniel Brandes would pose question after question and read on, on and on, stripping down everything to God but failing to wrap everything up again. I watched the thick twilight of this mystic philosophy coming on, and I had inside me a thousand different twilights. And seeing those twilights, I myself was those twilights, inside and out. Black blueness, in this twilight age of all disciplines, this twilight consciousness. We despise everything as we organize our persons around meaningless stars. How is it that we are so dull, dumb, empty?

Spiritual notes. University nauseated me. It was so tiresome that it made me want to take a shortcut and start living, start straightaway, without being ready. I was impatient about the future, however near the future might be. Overwhelmed by desperation to start writing that unwritten book. That unwritable book.

This paper soul of mine.

In my hands I held a black book. My own writing notebook. Trying not to make any noise, so as not to wake the Stefans, I undid its grey clasps. Closely-written pages rose and fell and rose again, until fresh, blank pages appeared. Virginal white. Dead pages.

I cast myself into the inky sea striated with thousands of pens, into a broader theme, squeezing my thoughts into a few phrases and so simplifying them.

My writing was still amateurish. I had just enough talent to get along. Terribly incomplete. I kept thinking, *Omit it, omit it.* Painful imperfection. Alien imperfection.

The book that I dreamed was faultless until I wrote it down. Once made, it was full of mistakes, errors of perspective or ignorance, moments of bad taste, weakness, sloppiness. When I write, I write badly. *Maybe,* I thought, *the great and perfect work is not even the one in my dream but the one I could never dream of creating.*

I started writing. *If you are still enough, clouds start to move. If you are quiet enough, your head becomes empty and dead. Even the rock, the cloud, and the tree would complain if, in addition to being a rock, a cloud, and a tree, they had to live.*

A futile project? Possibly. But I was drawn to futility. Because futility is inaccessible, indestructible, immovable. It is a true foundation. I wanted to become an expert at creating the inner lie, like everyone else had—at creating those imaginary figures, those sinister patterns of metaphor that engineered a sensation for the death of the sun and the hour of God. *Precisely this constitutes my material. Just as it stands. Partly true and partly completed. All that I have created is imperfect and unfinished. Everything is virtually in my hands. Everything is in my possession.*

And it was bitter consolation that here and now I could write everything down into this notebook because, on the one hand, I was most likely going to destroy it, so that no one would be able to read it. And, on the other hand, it was useless for me to be here, living this lifeway, it was useless for me to come here, and it was useless for me to understand the great secret. I had no desire to wait and see what would occur of its own accord. My research and my discovery of the tome had deprived me of that which I thought would give me strength. If I'd known, I wouldn't have begun to write.

The whole thing started off so nicely. It was still summer—July? August?—when I first discovered the tome. It no longer mattered.

Let Sleeping Dogs Lie. T.H.'s apartment was about as blank and empty as his new life. It had no furniture or clutter. Appealingly sombre. Mute.

An old banker's cheque for "John's TV" decorated one of the two rooms. It had belonged to Kerouac and had bounced in the fifties or sixties, I can't remember which, but was now encased in a small black frame that floated upon the layers of white paint, midwall. There were other collectable memorabilia, mostly a library of the No. Things like Herman Melville's *Bartleby, The Scrivener.* No yes-artists. None.

T.H. had all the symptoms of a Bartleby, inhabited, as he was, by a profound denial of the world. He would never be seen reading, not even a newspaper, while looking out a window upon a brick wall. Never drinking beer, or tea, or coffee. He'd never been anywhere, living as he did without an office, spending all his time not working. Never saying who he was, or where he came from, or whether he had any relatives in this world. The elusive T.H., with his obsession for protecting his private life, had every reason to justify his not writing but usually responded by spitting out a round "no."

Denial, refusal, silence. His poor face was the face of a man who wants people not to look at him. In his head, the language we all speak suffered mutilations, and those illiterate wounds of the symbols that joined us to him were either erased or deleted.

Being affected by this disease, this illness, this negative impulse or writing paralysis, T.H. entered a literary silence for more than twenty years. Though possessing a demanding conscience, he was never able to write again. I found his book in the abandoned apartment of this most secretive writer. A book on the art of refusal.

T.H.'s round, moon-shaped face, with its hooked nose, always had a faint look of disdain in its every feature. It was the face of someone who despises life and lives only to have something to despise. A cup of coffee, a cigarette, and the penetrating aroma of its smoke, T.H. sitting in the shadowy room of his apartment with eyes half closed—he wanted no more from life than his dreams of this.

He had come here for no reason, as was the case with everything in his life. And in a voice that trembled, and with a false smile, he would say: "I'm not from here anymore. I'm not from this world." And his weakness of will always began like this—that is, by being a weakness of the will to have a will. *We are lost if we acquire too much time for reflecting on ourselves*, I thought. *Because we become aware of so much that is dismal and wretched that at the sight of it, all the desire to organize it or hold it together departs from us.*

Later on, less cantankerous, sweeter and sadder, T.H. would say: "I don't get indignant, because indignation is for the strong; I don't resign myself, because resignation is for the noble; I don't keep silent, because silence is for the great. And I am neither strong nor noble nor great. I suffer and I dream. I complain because I am weak. My only regret is that I am not a child. I suffer and I complain, but I don't know if suffering is the general rule or if it is human to suffer. Why should I care if this is true or not? I am merely sad."

He needed a smoke in order to write and wasted most of his time searching for adjectives to describe that life. The ashtray consumed most of his cigarettes. He was addicted to silences, and so we engaged in conversations that often consisted of silences directed toward one another. He was suffused with sadness, mostly for himself. T.H. sat in his habitual posture, legs crossed, toe of the upper leg under the lower; I inevitably fell into the same posture.

T.H. had a job at the gas station, but it depressed him, filled him with all kinds of angry, painful excuses. This is where I had first met him, on one of his first backshifts. A semi-retired screenwriter, he was quick to tell you he wasn't a writer. He often said that he'd read absolutely everything and so preferred to reread what he'd already read or not bother at all. He hung around a hotel called the Lord Nelson, which he called the Hotel Abyss. He liked talking to the doormen of the Hotel Abyss, and other normal people around the city of Halifax. People who were unaware of their own unhappiness. People like me. He loved these people, despite everything, and often called them his "beloved garden-variety vegetables." He didn't like alcohol and was the type to go to the latest movie, whatever it was, with his ears stuffed full of plastic-wrapped bread crumbs to dampen the sound.

On occasion, I would visit this secretive writer in his final refuge. The space that T.H. had resigned himself to and that seemed to be growing smaller by the day. He thought it was just what he needed to be an arch writer of the No. Ready, as he was, to turn the lock on the whole world.

Not having the energy to start again at fifty-four, T.H. lived off what was left of his dwindling savings. He once told me that, during one of his back shifts at the gas station, he'd thrown a silver-foil wrapper to the ground and, as he was doing so, said very loudly:

"I throw away my life!"

Across the hall lived a woman who was blind, and T.H. would help her with her groceries and laundry. She was paranoid that T.H. was a thief, "just like everyone else." He said these were the last words she used before never speaking to him again.

This woman without sight, who lived across the hall, was crazy about Camus. A former scholar of that Sisyphean thinker, she'd often gotten T.H. to push the boulder by reading her the same passage from Camus' 1942 diary over and over again:

What does this sudden awakening mean, in this dark room, with the sounds of a city that has suddenly become foreign to me? And everything is foreign to me, everything, without a single person who belongs to me, with no hiding place to heal this wound. What am I doing here, what is the point of these smiles and gestures?

Trying to find a way of fleeing beyond God made T.H. a pessimist. After he lost God, his despairing gestures were different: bruised, silenced. He had sold his soul to God, which was much worse than selling his soul to the devil. "A divine enmity" were the words this elusive writer had used then. A divine enmity had forced his belief to secularize itself into nothing but nerves and indecisions.

Once, on the way out of a late-night movie, I think it was a film directed by Xavier Dolan, I asked T.H. what he thought about it. "It was like taking Viagra in order to feel something and feeling nothing as you count the numb strokes going in and out, in and out. All the appearance of a pre-climax without the climax; an anti-climax."

T.H. created an inner aristocracy for himself—an aristocratic attitude for an aristocratic soul. In particular, his hands were the light-fingered hands of a consummate aristocrat. His hands were ten human fingers without the human. He put them in warm, soapy water early in the morning. The polished pink shields of nails flashed on these white hands with long, gentlemanly fingers, with which he shook his cigarettes. Then, after dressing them attentively in soft leather gloves, he cradled them in the pockets of his warm coat and went for a stroll. He'd walk around with his jacket securely fastened, his hands in his pockets. He'd cast his Bartlebian shadow all the way to the Hotel Abyss.

His hands were made for light gestures, not for work. After working at the gas station, those once-white, tapered, manicured fingers smelling of expensive cologne were brownish grey and covered with abrasions. He lay them in hideous heaps. Their ulcerated skin was caked with uncleanness. Their tips, repulsively flattened, bore the yellow excrescences of calluses. The nails were broken and lacerated. Dried blood was black under the bends of the joints. The ruthless and gigantic fingers were from another world, the world of work, which he had always, until now, found some way or another to avoid.

T.H. was accustomed to thinking of himself as a mental reality and of others as merely physical realities: "I'm going to leave," he told me, in a humiliated way. "One of these days I'm going to take a taxi with the last of my savings and leave this dunghill behind. I'll tell the cabby to drive, and the cabby will drive. Once I get there, I'll pay the cabby and walk straight into the woods, the way a sick animal who's ready to die would. Then, I'll find a nice spot in those woods and strip down to nothing, because what is the use of clothes there? Then, I'll crouch down in the fetal position. And there I'll stay, not 'till my death, but 'till everyone else's."

That was the last I saw of T.H. He vanished after he said this. Saying he would return in a few hours, he disappeared. That T.H.—who had suddenly and without reason abandoned his wife and home twenty years ago, only so he could lead a solitary existence somewhere else, hoping to be an unbroken failure of a writer—had once again abandoned more than just literature.

Since it would make no sense to publish what should not be published, I sent what I could find of his unfinished work, *The Art of Refusal*, to the Brautigan Library in Vancouver,

Washington, America—a sort of abortion library that would take any unpublished manuscripts you sent them and archive them according to the Mayonnaise System so that ordinary people, readers mostly, could be inspired by these artists without works.

I probably went against his will by doing so. But T.H. was no longer there, not even for the art of refusal. He really was a recalcitrant writer without books. His one book was a book by someone who had declined to write. A book without text. I reproduce it here:

(eighty paragraphs of blank writing on blank pages)

The Undersigned. It was a brown quarto-sized notebook. A diary. As part of a protest against on-campus mental health services, people were raising awareness by leaving personal, though thoroughly anonymous, accounts all over campus. The campus newspapers called them "the suicide diaries" and provided detailed instructions on how to turn them in to the proper authorities. Some of the suicide diaries contained their author's death notes. Others were merely a form of expression. No bodies were connected to any of the notebooks.

The first suicide diary that I found, hidden in the lining of a long coat on a bus bench near campus, contained a death note. I decided to keep it. It read as follows.

I was born dead, I lived dead, and I enter death already dead.

I am a cadaverous person. The persistence of my corpse gives testimony to the notion that death is not the end. We, the undersigned, in each moment of our lives, are both a reflection and an effect of what surrounds us. Composed of living cells and in a state of permanent dissolution: I am made of death.

My dead body is a putrefying corpse. And for me, my "I" is the "death" symbol, that biological minus in my formulas. The formula of a diagnosis. Cotard delusion or, as I prefer to call it, walking corpse syndrome.

You may think because I'm partly alive that I'm constantly praying for the sound to return or else for the image to return, and that's where you're wrong. You must confront the fact that this person, the undersigned, the living-dead person, is actually dead.

I analyzed my will to death. And from there, I gradually denied the existence of everything else. Of God. Of soul, of spirit. Of the body and the mind. By denying the existence of these things, by denying their necessity to my existence, it was as if I'd already paralyzed parts within me and had entered the last form of living. "Within me is not" is all that I can think to say to myself. "Within me is not." Because I can carry no more weight, I can say to myself, "Within me is not."

To think that thought is still inside my cavernous, hollowed-out skull... It is imaginable that my skull should turn out empty when I'm operated on by the coroner. The empty skull—the brain at its most useful.

But I found my hunger cure and no longer need to eat. The main thing is that as soon as I came upon this fantasy cure, I immediately wrote it down here in this notebook, for which I have expended much energy trying to devise newer and newer hiding places. I did find a good hiding place for it, although I'm not sure that it's the best. Perhaps the best was just keeping it with me at all times, as I've done up 'till now. I've found my hunger cure and no longer need to eat. For the function of a dead mouth isn't for food, nor is it for kissing or speaking. It is for silence.

That she would starve herself, I thought, and shut the notebook.

The blue octavo notebook was different from the brown quarto-sized notebook.

I began to wonder, after stumbling upon this second notebook, somewhere in an athletics field, whether it would be useful to humanity if I compiled a digest of their dreams—the dreams written in these lost notebooks. Those dreams of those fatigued by the journeys they never made and never would make.

This blue notebook was an incomplete chronicle of unhealed mental wounds. As I turned over the pages of this notebook, I realized that these suicide diaries were an indestructible monster. The essence of this monster would remain. I read those strange pages, following the intellectual anxiety of their author.

I repeated the words that were spoken. My thoughts circled obsessively around in my head. The beginnings, middles, and ends of voices. Reliving the ephemera of one moment before I began another. Making sure that I absorbed all that was pleasant or unpleasant about them. I spoke to myself, sometimes out loud, sometimes not. Because if I hear myself speaking out loud, the ears with which I hear myself speaking out loud do not listen to me in the same way as the invisible, inner mental ear with which I think those thoughts. Those thoughts of other people's understanding of me that are made up of so many misunderstandings, so many errors in their hearing. I'll never know the delight of being understood, and will only ever feel the desire to be understood, the want to be understood.

Even the thought of my impending manipulation of hook and noose, a thought that I have, oddly, never had before now, cannot keep me from smiling. Oh the tedium of being. Life certainly is a murderer.

I feel uncomfortable where I am and uncomfortable where I am going. I failed life even before I lived it, because even as I dreamed it, I failed to see its appeal. I've dreamed a lot. Now I'm tired from dreaming but not tired of dreaming. No one tires of dreaming, because to dream is to forget. To forget our perception, which is a kind of overturned dream.

My habits of isolation make me a solitary image. The presence of another person immediately slows down my thinking. When I'm alone, I can come up with endless ideas. But all this disappears the moment I'm confronted by another human being. I lose all my intelligence, I lose the power of speech, and after a while all I feel like doing is sleeping. Yes, talking to people makes me feel like sleeping. The whole idea of being forced into contact with someone oppresses me. The idea of any social obligation blocks up my thoughts for whole days and I sleep badly because of it. And yet, when the reality of it does come, it is utterly insignificant and never worth all the fuss.

It happens again and again and yet I never learn.

I asked myself if all the effort I put into isolating and elevating myself was worth it, if the failure I made of myself to achieve my living in life falsely and in dreams was worth it, was religiously worth the trouble, for I wasn't fortunate enough to have been raised atheist in a secular society. And even if I know that it was, I am weighed down by the feeling that it wasn't worth the effort and never will be.

Ah, the whole apparatus is no more than a piece of rope that works on one simple, ruthless principle. A noose at one end, with just enough space for my head, the other tied firmly to the top of the wood beam.

In the stupid depths of my thought, deep down, I think, the saddest part of me is the least real part, and my greatest tragedies occurred in my own idea of myself. The idea of myself as I'm writing this.

A not entirely clear-cut person, I thought. *Even for me.* But I could really believe he wanted to choke or self-guillotine himself with the solitary charity of his cord.

The undersigned of these notebooks shaped their lives by becoming mysteries to others. They almost unintentionally summoned from themselves a single, dry, factual, tragic story.

The Fear of Failure. From a drawer in my desk I produced a blue folder with a large label on which was written: "Archive of Abandoned Books." Inside—among the fragments, chance finds, sudden recollections of books, lives, texts, or individual sentences that gradually enlarged the dimensions of the labyrinth without centre—were fifty or so quarto sheets on which in red ink I had written of the books that had been abandoned; books that, in effect, never went beyond the first page. I read the words on some of those sheets, read them again and again until I knew them almost by heart. They read something like this:

A human living without a why is destined to fail. Letting-be is the most tiring of forms, because the human form takes on the abandoned shell or the carcass of an existing form and so becomes a tragic type of misanthrope.

The archive was a labyrinth that lacked a centre. There was no overall unity in it, for there are as many people as there are ways of abandonment. It wasn't even simple to hit on a true sentence that joined them in their endemic disease.

What matters, I thought, *is that they wrote it.* With happiness denied, all of them were writing their way back into the anonymous health of normal life.

I stopped attending school. My short-term loans were almost gone. Being paid by other people—family, friends, banks, the government—was somehow disturbing. It was money gained by another person's efforts. So I resisted. I fled. Because I was exhausted. I couldn't live off of others forever. I couldn't live forever. I couldn't. I could not. I could. I.

Period.

Suicide or Coffee? Bürger interpreted my sarcasm as sincerity. For a second he fixated on me with a squinting, slightly malicious eye, but then he relaxed a little and gave me a metaphysical smile. He was knocked out by this comment of mine, raising his eyebrows quizzically, and then sucked back into it when I repeated it.

The interrupted conversation is a failure.

"They both offer hope: suicide and coffee. One immediate and the other long and protracted." I shouted this and Bürger nodded, having heard the important words and so understanding now that I was referring to Camus's dilemma, engraved on the very wood of the ancient surface of our table.

He's drinking a beer, I'm drinking coffee.

I barely touch mine, just sip it, a very unpleasant drink, as coffee drunk out of a wine glass usually is, but still I sipped it so that I could remain there for a few more hours. A fragrance of lukewarm mud rose from the slumbering coffee. They had not only run out of mugs but also utensils. The sight of meat being cut with the pair of scissors from a Swiss Army knife was enough evidence for me that the world depended on presentation.

Bürger drained his glass. Ordered another. And went on talking while looking through me. He had graduated, finally, after a decade of being a dropout. He was a tall, solid man of thirty or thirty-one with steel-framed glasses on his nose and a well-trimmed, spade-shaped beard. He cut an altogether masculine figure with an air of immediately impressive melancholy. And here he was telling me that his novel was all planned out, and, at this point, just needed to be written. He told me this in his cold-blooded Canadian-American manner, while sporting, on that pessimistic Dionysian chest of his, a T-shirt that affirmed a double negative: [no/no].

Only a very early version of the first chapter of his novel had been published, which constituted one-third of the entire work. This one-third still needed revisions, Bürger said, not to mention he needed enough funding to continue writing those last two-thirds. Instead, the end of the story was being—he tapped his pointer finger on his right temple while saying this—written and rewritten, day after day, in his head.

The novel was the spiritual cousin of Kafka's *Amerika*, Bürger told me. He proudly explained that in the same way *Amerika* opens with an eager, optimistic immigrant happily spying the Statue of Liberty (which holds aloft a sword instead of a torch), a strange little narrative shift from our world into a surreal world is present in *Kanada*. Winnipeg's "Golden Boy" also holds a sword, but, more radically, the entire city core is surrounded by a massive wall of black metal designed to keep its denizens downtown. Because, so he reasoned, a metaphorical wall has always surrounded us in the Canadian imagination—an invisible wall that we built in our heads.

I wasn't listening, not even hearing, because pointless music was being played loudly through the bar speakers, and I tended to be suspicious of anything I hadn't written myself. Instead, I found myself thinking, as a person of ideals, that perhaps my greatest aspiration didn't go beyond occupying this chair at this table in this secret bar, The Burrow, listening to Bürger's elevator pitch for *Kanada*.

The subterranean workers of The Burrow were now running to the upper level to turn off the tiny neon cactus sign, which meant that the password we'd received by text message ("pomegranate tiger") was no longer valid; was no longer "pomegranate tiger." It would be something else tomorrow. The secret bar, which was really just the developed basement of a Turkish lounge, The Ottoman Café, no longer existed when it no longer had a password to exist for. We were not there, nobody was there, yet the secret bar was at capacity, and so no more people could join our being not there.

The main band, The Body, was playing a real hardcore gig, a secret show in the secret bar. They were an American experimental sludge-metal-punk duo, the Canadian-American explained to me. I'd seen the duo come into the bar with burlap sacks over their heads.

When the two performers started playing, I gazed at them, then at the mass of people, then at the band again, as their music communicated its ruthless melancholy. Their music incapacitated me, drugged me, defeated me. The singer—tattooed lips, tattooed arms—would scream into the microphone with a severe and terminally exhausted expression. The microphone was programmed to distort his voice so his words were almost indecipherable. I heard only odd phrases, such as, "Alone all the way" and "Darkness surrounds us." The pink-haired drummer stood at the back and, in a peculiar, quite unbearable racket, thrashed at his drums while staring straight ahead.

A thick veil shrouded everything:

The music, the venue, the mass of young faces; the dim light, the volume of noise; the dense crowd of people, the stench, and all those dazed, empty sad eyes everywhere; the groups of perspiring dancers humming in chorus with the singer, in an ever-growing sea of glassy eyes, eyes that did not seem to see anything amid that exhaustion of human seaweed. Like eels in a bowl they became so entangled with one another that it seemed as though they might never escape this music.

The singer continued to scream until, finally, he stopped. Not at the end of the song, but somewhere in the middle, abruptly. He removed his guitar and left the stage to seek out a drink that he must have felt he'd earned by tolerating this seething crowd. His clothing revealed the corrosive effect of prolonged poverty.

I tried to explain to the cold-blooded Canadian-American that I was exhausted, too tired to unfasten the clasps of the now-tattered book in my hands, where I had set down, in its pieces of paper, a description of my ideal for his novel—a novel that I had experienced as nothing but an endless void and boredom, and so my edits were mostly childish doodles. But Bürger was, by this point, as lost to the world as all the flopping, sack-like bodies around us. Sleeping the deep sleep of sin without sin. Tucking my black notebook under my arm, I stood up, ascended the stairs, and left the secret bar through the Turkish lounge's front door.

Hope? None. I no longer believed in a favourable outcome and I did not comfort myself with the thought that any such consultation was to be had. I was utterly resigned to whatever might happen and resisted any hysterical hope of resolution. *I experience life as apocalypse and cataclysm.*

DREAM MATERIAL: Second Phase

The Postscripts of Things Lost

Human Words That Will Never Be. I have to give up. Nothing's coming. I'm here. But nothing's happening. You have to really sit there and believe yourself. Tell yourself. You have to intend.

Writing has become more and more boring because my existence is so utterly uneventful. I sit down and wait for my computer to turn on, put my hands on the keyboard. When I moved back in with my parents, the door to my old room was different, the door to my old life in that room was different. Different house, different room, different life.

Years of sitting, staring into my computer, voluntarily reading submissions from all over the world, working the never-ending slush pile. Only to be on the other side of the rejection. I've come to realize that everyone dreams of becoming a writer, of the name of a story they'll write one day, when it finally does come out.

I type "Rej." again and hit Enter on the decline option.

I see another paper-clip icon with a PDF extension. I double-click it. Another submission.

Collective member Captain_Ahab said: "I don't know about this one. What do you guys think? Please include feedback."

Form: Fiction
Submitted by: Sasha Visser on 02/13/2018
Title
"The Worst"
Cover Letter
Dear Sir or Madam,
I was born in Montreal and currently live abroad working multiple jobs. I am a recent graduate of Concordia University and have been published in several CanLit Magazines and have competed in multiple reading series competitions.

My piece "The Worst" is a pessimistic fiction short story about the relationship between cynicism and hope, a topic that I've been thinking a lot about recently and one I've found a special passion for.
**I do apologize in advance for my grammar mechanics. I do have a nonverbal learning disability.*

Intersectional identities: Queer fat femme with temporary immigration status and disabling chronic mental illness.

I get up from my thinking and move away from the screen, lean my head all the way back, and stretch my neck. I try to calculate how long I've been at the computer. I log off the submission platform and go to the living room to watch TV and wait for my parents to come home.

Each day, it seems impossible that there will come another day, and perhaps there really is no other day, only this single one, or not even this.

And the same holds true regarding the stories. There might be ten, a hundred, a thousand million stories submitted to me, day after day, week after week, month after month, year after year, and it's as if among all those stories only a single one were true, or not even one, so that the succession of days one after another, or the stack of stories mounting up one on top of the other, neither of them holds up, neither exists. I cannot rely on them, cannot rely on anything.

I hate reading. I feel a kind of anticipatory tedium at the prospect of all those unread pages.

It's always like this with stories: they've already ended. There's always a problem with these stories. I'm always being shown some story that isn't a story, never was one. Even if it turns out to be a story, each one is the same. It's not that there are no stories. There are only ever stories. There are billions of stories. To say that there are no stories when we are made only of stories is an impossible thing to understand. But no matter how detailed or how well-explained these stories are, we lose the essence of the story itself, the one true story, while we live among billions of stories.

There's nothing more to be done, I thought. Everyone who hesitantly liberated themselves, believing, if nothing else, in the invincibility of their weaknesses, in their intersectional identities, everyone who found the use of false names somehow managed to monumentalize destructiveness as victims of regrettable accidents—LGBTQ, Indigenous, refugees, women, minorities, the mentally ill, those with disabilities. I, the absent antagonist, who controls the machinery of goodness, can become only a fanatic obsessed with people who organize themselves around their weakness, who have a cause I can only ever support from the periphery. Whose alien transparency leaves me with a sense of dead ambitions or sham intentions. I include them without resembling them and all around me things begin to turn serious.

I let it go. What's the point of sharing this with anyone, of driving yourself mad with explanation? I'm ashamed because I can't really imagine truly explaining to somebody why I'm researching failure with such persistence, such obsessiveness, when I don't know myself why I'm doing it. It keeps changing as the days and the weeks go by. In the beginning I knew, or at least I was convinced I knew, but then it all became even more obscure, and as for today, I stand here with hundreds and hundreds of books, documents, films, and photographs. If I were to ask myself why, everything would grow completely dark at once. I have nothing to do or to even think of doing.

And nothing is worse than being alone and waiting in the dark. Waiting, in that maternal silence, to be reborn, to be given another chance, but this time as the afterbirth, as the purple placenta that was thrown out by the doctor, or buried under a tree in a German forest, or seasoned and eaten in sacred ceremony, or used as the flag for a great pharaoh of ancient Egypt.

Perhaps I will have the qualities that I need if I'm going to rise to the top. The qualities of an upstart. There are many upstarts, and stupidly they cling to what they have attained, and that is nothing deep. All human culture is but an attempt at something unattainable, something that far transcends our powers of realization. Upstarts call what is grey, quiet, hard, and humble their attainment. And so, if I would like to remain in good health, I'll need my own spirit of initiative. Yes, it's clear now: the spirit of initiative is what I need. Because there are no graveyards here in the suburbs, and I'm afraid yesterday's corpse—that is, who I am today—will be ash in the urn of tomorrow.

Forever farewell, restless river.

Heteroclite Accumulations

After pouring a full glass of mushroom wine, I set down the bottle on my writing desk and raise the glass to my lips. Sniffing the liquid, I wrinkle my nose. There's the stink of ozone about it, and my first hesitant sip is even more acrid than I expected. The seventy-proof mushroom blooms hot in my belly. But the taste isn't nearly as disagreeable as I'd thought it would be. There's a faint bitterness underneath the pine-needle and alcohol sting. The second sip is less of a shock, less nauseating.

The sun seems to be lighting up a crime, this bright, cold sun, shining through the late-November clouds. And as the sun shines in this deep dead of the shoulder season, I'm wasting away in semi-active idleness preparing an already postponed PhD defence that I may never actually give. Likely won't give. And will never be able to give again because this is my last chance at obedience—my last chance to guarantee the survival of my thesis, according to the committee.

The dissertation committee, the faculty in front of which I'm supposed to stand in rigorous and sustained critical vigilance, comprises three or five incredulous and long-faced examiners, each of whom will have an opportunity to thoroughly scrutinize my completely inconceivable thesis on the illusion of language generated by language's natural exercise for two or six incomprehensible hours that will feel something like days or weeks. But since I won't be there to present it, the committee will simply move on to another PhD defence. And I'm sure the next thesis will be a much better thesis than my thesis or at least a less boring thesis than my thesis. Because nothing is more boring than your own thesis. Especially my own.

I take another, bolder swallow. The taste is becoming familiar now, somewhat, *somewhat,* pleasant.

The lights on the mountain are still glowing, which means the small hydroelectric generator's battery bank hasn't quite run out of power yet. Since the death of Naveen's mother, I've taken over as full-time operator. I'm supposed to be constantly monitoring and adjusting the generator for the neighbouring community—people who pay a vacancy tax for their houses to stay empty—using a personal-computer-based control system, a regrettably complicated interface that Naveen rigged up himself so that everyone could live sustainably off-grid here in the Selkirk Mountains on the extreme West Arm of Kootenay Lake in the Southern Interior of British Columbia.

I'm sure a blackout will happen soon. When a micro-hydro setup has been in continuous operation since '95, like this one has, well, that's twenty-five-year-old turbines out in the field.

I glance out the window. Winter rain is falling now, and the glass is becoming more and more clouded. I inhale the scent of the glowing gas stove behind me: a melancholic, lonely odour, the sweet body odour of old wood burning.

It never occurs to me to remove myself completely from this guesthouse, what I've begun to call the *khôra*. The arrangement gives us some proper space during a formless interval of our relationship—I've been staying here, in abeyance, since the funeral. In fact, I haven't been monitoring the generator, which is very close to the guest house, nearly enough. But I could always just go and check the meters in the powerhouse, simply go and check that the volume of available water and the turbine's discharge rate are both being accurately measured by the generator's automation process.

"During the autumn rainfall, the output power will need to be adjusted from minimum to maximum water flow," Naveen told me, months and months ago. I was walking with him along a steep slope near a fast-moving stream. He explained to me precisely how a small-scale hydro system was the best solution, given the amount of energy everyone in the area needed, making sure to point out that these kinds of systems—which he sometimes called micro-hydro systems, other times run-of-stream hydro systems, and still other times low-impact hydro systems—usually consisted of an enclosed waterwheel or turbine, which are made to spin by jets of high-velocity water.

He went on to tell me precisely how the water was taken from the stream and moved downslope to the turbine through a long pipe called a penstock. How water flowing through the penstock picks up speed, and how it's then directed at the turbine's blades by nozzles.

"So," he'd said, not turning his head to look at me, "the turbine spins continuously, as long as there's water to drive it. The turbine is connected to an electrical generator, and the electricity is then available for running appliances or charging batteries. And the spent water is returned to the stream."

The glass is empty, and the buzz in my head is gentle behind my eyes, so I pour myself some more. Eventually, I wrap myself in a warm blanket, step into my hiking boots with the worn-down heels, and make my round. Just to be done with it. Just to stop worrying that there might be a blackout. Because if there is a blackout, the people who are still around to check on the empty houses are sure to complain about it to Naveen—who has been too depressed to do anything whatsoever. And if that happens then Naveen, in his ill humour, is likely to tell me to leave the guest house, or if you like, the khôra, I've been staying in since we stopped speaking and I had to move out of the main house.

And the thing is, I couldn't leave the guesthouse even if I needed to, not yet anyway, and enter what I've begun to call "the chaos." I couldn't leave Nelson even to attend my own dissertation defence because the ferry workers are on strike. Not only are these labourers preventing people from crossing Kootenay Bay but also the Pass. And since they're blocking the only way into the city and the only way out of the city, I can't expect to leave until the strike is over and done with, until the labourers are given their living wage and stop with this nonsense. So, until that happens, I'll do what Naveen wants me to do.

Flaccid compromise.

Which is to say, I check to see if there's anything obstructing the river system that's supplying the turbine. This spot, just outside the engine room, where waterpower is transformed into the rotational force that drives the generator—into the blades of the runner, the heart of the turbine, which captures the most possible energy from the water—is relatively shallow and so has a lot of weeds. The trash racks, several grates, prevent these weeds and other debris from entering the turbine itself. But the trash racks are plugged and I can see that these weeds are restricting water from passing through to the turbines. Without pause, I uproot the weeds and let their bodies be carried downstream. I uproot the weeds that are plugging up the trash rack until there are no more weeds left to plug up anything.

Then I unlock the door to the small room housing the generator.

The most critical information the system requires is an accurate and constant indication of the powerhouse's water level. The manual control system is simple enough: a motor used to adjust the gates, to control the flow of water that enters the turbine, but the additional components, the various electrically operated control devices, are beyond me. All I know is that the main generator breaker somehow synchronizes the generator with the rest of the grid. And that the limit switch, another component, prevents the control system from burning out the motor. The other device is a four-position switch used to determine the gates' various critical locations. Naveen meticulously labeled these positions in writing: "gates fully closed," "gates at speed no load," "gates at seventy percent," and "gates fully open."

I switch the gates to "fully open" and immediately head back to the guest house. On my way, I decide to peek inside Naveen's mother's tawdry little hovel by the stream. The place smells shut away. Like mildew and dust and time. It's crammed from wall to wall with clutter. I have trouble imagining how she navigated it in her wheelchair.

I pause, feeling new and awkward in the place, and look at the floor—at the careless scatter of empty tin cans and empty bottles and makeshift altars and what look like shrines. She fervently devoted herself to the sewing of bags, and every corner of the house is filled with examples of her handicraft. She'd made them for the Love of Shiva Boutique until she started to lose her vision.

The house is entirely without a stair because it wasn't until Naveen's maternal grandparents passed away that his mother inherited their fortune. All through Naveen's childhood they'd been poor. Day after day, his mother would pitifully drag herself up the stairs of whatever rundown house they could afford on disability assistance.

After I return to the guest house, having avoided the possibility of a blackout by unplugging the powerhouse's weedy turbine, I realize I can't stop myself from staring down at my hands. I haven't paused to look at them closely for a long time. It's as though I'm suddenly *noticing* them. I can't recall the last time that I did.

I sit down, very still, in the broken-down armchair. All the springs are shot, and I sink several inches. The chair squeaks and pops angrily when I lean over to retrieve a document from my briefcase.

I've written a lot. Too much. I try to clear my head and focus. To decide what might steer me back on course. To turn my frame of mind into a firm resolve. And the more this resolve hardens in me, the more it resembles a kind of secret pleasure for my writing to go horribly awry.

I no longer know how to do anything with these documents of inert and sterile material. These documents are more like monuments than text. Monuments of a language. Language has no other function but description, so goes my thesis on post-deconstructionism: it no longer has a constitutive function. We are all in language, in the sense that language exists in our mind and we are in our minds all our human lifespan, but what we say with language isn't always real.

So causality is built into language, though only the left side of our brain can process this language. Because the right side can't comprehend anything besides affects, we tend to become overly reliant on this interpreter as we age out of our child minds, i.e., the left hemisphere. This interpreter of language and so of logic. Of the words that we say to each other. Of the language inventory we keep of ourselves. Our abnormalities. Our irregularities. Our, if you will, heteroclite accumulations. For instance, I frequently say "no matter what" about Naveen's behaviour. I say "no matter what" again and again: *No matter this, no matter that, no matter what, I'll be here for you, it will get better, etc.* And this has only ever proved useless and abusive—never *really* an intention, just *supposedly* real. No emotion, just words.

I am a delayed image of myself.

It's at least preserved, I think, and shake my head in disbelief. Even if I don't make it to my dissertation defence, my thesis is at least preserved in this or that description. In a sense, everything I've thought to describe and describe again is conserved in this or that description, now preserved in this thesis. All my decisions are still present in their complicated combinations, but they have turned inert and sterile and so have I. *But the material isn't simply inert*, I think, *and neither am I.* In a sense, I am my own thesis. These descriptions are a necessary material requiring a certain labour, which also makes me necessary.

Like the ferry workers are necessary labourers because their labour is necessary. Even as a child, I could see the necessity the government chooses to overlook. Those people who worked the ferry when I used to make my annual trip from Nelson to Grey Creek—first to visit my estranged grandfather and his partner and then later to visit the grave that replaced him—they're the same people working the ferry now.

So I remain content with simply reworking old descriptions in my thesis. It's like pushing the food around on one's plate. I'm content with placing myself between an unsatisfying first description and the second description that rectifies the first.

A decision exists. I sigh and give the micro muscles around my eyes and the cranial nerves of my face a pressure-point massage. In as much as you can judge these oceanic matters, something like a decision must exist. And because Voltaire smiled like a Voltaire when he wrote, so too must I smile like myself when I write.

The whole problem is choosing a particular decision to reformulate a particular language: the particular language of this thesis. This thesis that I am. What changes vastly from one description to another is only the language that is used to describe what's supposed to be real—for example, to formulate in Heraclitean language the structure of a decision that appears more or less in the Heraclitean material. And in the Heraclitean material, thought completely holds to the worn-out Heraclitean type of decision, which says that for a given thing there corresponds one contrary thing and one alone.

And so my first error is obviously remaining unable to imagine something besides a Heraclitean relation to that one contrary thing and one thing alone, this correspondence being the most significant and noteworthy of all Heraclitean phenomena. Because this one contrary thing that we're all supposed to have is just the infinite multiplication of circles. Circles of decision. More specifically, different kinds of decisions previously joined, brought into contact, like Naveen and me. Once brought into contact, we were not two people. We were one person—an enigma whose solution could be discovered only with each other's help—before we completely abandoned that previous union, our previous intention to stay together not as two people but one person. We might possibly join together afresh later, but for now we are merely resistant. Suspended.

And it is in this relinquishment and seizing of one another, Naveen and I, that we can really believe we're witnessing a real decision being made. Our sustained resistance will have to give way, and when we've been lowered from this state of suspension, from this region of inertness to that of attraction, it will be by yet another disturbance. So we must watch how we once again seek each other out: attract, seize, destroy, devour, consume, and then emerge from this intimate union in renewed, novel, and unexpected shapes.

Because, I think, no one will love him if I don't. And no one will fuck him if I don't.

I slip into a fever dream. I hear the burrowing of busy animals under the earth, where I imagine night and day are one. And whatever sensation was once in my hands seems to have moved to my teeth. Each tooth makes contact with every other tooth when I clench my jaw. A piece of calculus chips off and slides down my throat, which has become dry and constricted by my increased anxiety. I walk to the empty kitchen sink and almost frantically pull back my lips to see my swollen gums reflected back at me in the scraped-up stainless steel. They've receded, some portions more than others, some right down to the root bed; an irreversible change, like so many more to come.

I call my thesis advisor to tell her I can't make it.

"Again?" I can hear her disappointment.

"Yes," I say.

She keeps talking. Administrative nonsense, taking up a lot of my time. I stare at the receiver. "You can't go back to school and become a—"

I miss this part because the line goes dead. I must have hung up on her. *No*, I think, *it's just that the blackout finally happened.*

Sounds are ringing in my ears. Things are stirring and bustling. Things are glittering and dancing before my eyes. Things

I'd long dreamed of are being conveyed to my mouth: "These are people—my thesis advisor and the whole damn dissertation committee—with whom I had nothing to do."

I set the phone back on the receiver and realize that it's one of those afternoons where I can't write. I can't think and I can't write and I don't feel much like getting drunk alone in the absolute dark on mushroom wine, either. Naveen and I found the mushroom during one of our hikes through the Doukhobor community. It supposedly cures mental illness, which, according to medieval belief, is caused by a fly entering people's heads.

Naveen wanted me to eat the mushroom and then urinate into his mouth so he could experience just the hallucinogenic properties without the poison. I immediately suggested we parboil it, dry it out, pulverize it into a powder, and then distill it into an alcohol and so avoid drinking each other's urine.

Instead of writing, I head into the city, where Naveen has been almost as obsessively rolling boulders to form small sitting circles as I have been preparing for a dissertation defence that I will never be able to make.

I follow the broad path that leads to the burial grounds. Here I encounter an animal, one stray dog. It smiles at me with all its keen and ruthless canine teeth. I feel its resentment as it slips into the rainy forest.

These alterations Naveen has been making—moving all the gravestones and leveling the ground—seem more in harmony with the nature of the land. Each time he moves and dispenses with yet another rough and rugged gravestone, he levels the ground right away and sows snow roses.

It has made a solemn impression on me. But these well-conceived, well-executed monuments of his, these sitting circles that Naveen has scattered about, do not show where people are buried. It doesn't really matter where they're buried, I suppose. After death, unlike in life, we are all one and all equal.

Not superior, not inferior.

When I find him, he's nearly finished constructing another sitting circle, unable to break his superbly claustrophobic focus. And I realize that he doesn't need to be put back on his feet: he remains what he is. It is I, on the other hand, and I alone, who needs to be placed back in myself.

Equivocal Intrigue

I'm a minor character in Jack Chiang's story. I knew him once, as schoolboys do. Even then I never really knew him—never really knew the person he was before he became the person things seemed to happen to.

Since then, I've collected the magazine images, watched the videos, read the articles. I've spent a long time looking at the face I'd known but now would not and I feel all the jealousy is gone or else it is so far away that I no longer think of it as mine.

Cleared of all these archival materials which have cluttered up the shelves, my home office seems vast. It is possible to know someone for years, decades even, learning little by little how to avoid personal questions and anything of real importance, but hope remains that some day, in different circumstances, one could talk about such things, pose such questions. A hope that can persist for years until a single, brutal act, like Jack Chiang's death, makes it clear that it is too late, the hope for a deep and meaningful relationship will never happen.

Devastated, and with a trace of bitterness, I glance at the boxes piled on the floor of the office and then proceed in hastily reopening what I have just successfully packed away.

I'm looking at a series of photographs. The first one shows Jack Chiang at the age of eleven surrounded by his family: younger brother and sister and immigrant parents, the father Chinese and the mother Welsh. Each bears a vacuous expression. Above the photo, the *StarMetro*'s headline reads: "Electric Company Says No to Bereavement Damages. Family of Terminally Ill Father at a Loss."

Jack's father was front-page material, a provincial icon. The photo was taken only three months after the man's diagnosis. Fear on his face. He would soon die of leukemia two months later. In the schoolyard that day Jack Chiang's father died, many years ago, I looked at my classmate and felt I knew what he was thinking, but I could not have.

I can only wonder why the picture of this family of five, soon to be four, is so remarkably disagreeable to me.

Jack Chiang's face in the second snapshot is startlingly like his face in the first. It's impossible to guess his age in this one. Possibly because his left eye is swollen. The picture is one of pretense, insincerity, fatuousness. With a mixture of repugnance and fascination, I detect pride in his expression, as if he felt that the swollen eye were revealing his inner essence, deep and profound, for this obscene photograph. By this point he'd already created Killdoom, a seven-piece band.

The family of the first photograph has been replaced by a rehabilitation-focused community—a revolving troop of musicians, filmmakers, and designers who use their music and visual art as therapy for their addictions. Strangely unpleasant, this handsome young man. But something has changed in his face, or at least in what I see there. It's a pictograph of something baffling. A shameless celebration of being mortal.

The final photograph is the most monstrous of all because it was taken by a world-famous designer who recruited the experimental punk collective from Canada to compose, record, and produce the score for a men's fashion showcase of a French luxury brand. I didn't understand the chemistry.

Again, here, there is no expression whatsoever in Jack Chiang. Just blunt virility. The picture has a genuinely chilling, foreboding quality. The more I examine his face the more I feel an indescribable, unspeakable horror creeping over me. He isn't smiling and his arms are crossed. His hands are tightly clenched into fists. He's tense and impersonal. Nervy, hypnotic, shirtless, tattooed. *Pain Olympics,* in gothic typography, has been inked in the little place where the collarbones meet, just below the dip of his suprasternal notch. There's more ink on his left arm, and running over his bellybutton are the words

Laughing
At The - Navel - System

In these pictures, Jack Chiang is nothingness. And yet he's perfect nothingness. So intense, his watching, his observation, his unceasing. "I can do anything," the artist who is needed by no one but himself seems to suggest as he stands there. "At any time and for any reason, I can do anything."

In 2020, after just four years as a band, half of the Killdoom gang died. I pin on the wall opposite me the faces of those pictured in the death notices. I can't process the fact that their deaths came so quickly. Can't process the fact that they poisoned not only themselves but an entire music venue of people. Especially given their miserable membership in this rehabilitation-focused community. Jack Chiang's adolescent trauma, the loss of his father to cancer of the blood, isn't enough to justify his art for me. And so I just look at those death notices on the wall opposite. I'm not about to come up with anything resembling sense or reason. Sometimes, there is simply no sense and no reason.

He was a dropout. And from what I could tell, he only ever used his good name to disgrace it. What it stood for. Jack Chiang used each of his failed projects as a launching point, used each new low to propel himself another step up, to the next band. Until his early twenties, when he hit rock bottom. After he'd taken massive amounts of psychedelic drugs and poured that experience into his art, his closest friends and family rehabilitated him.

His uncle, Victor Chiang—the president and CEO of an upscale construction company and owner of several restaurants in Calgary—suggested that his nephew become an electrical engineer like his father and offered to pay for the schooling. He told him he'd be sure to get him a job after he finished the program. Jack Chiang used his training in self-importance to turn his uncle's power on its head and use it as an aegis for yet another band. Yet another broken promise. Yet another violation of trust that would benefit only him and his project. Because he had no interest in giving up on his art.

Jack Chiang was willing to think in extremes and name them—former acts with which he'd been associated were indication enough of that: Starvation Cage, Hamas. And so it was no surprise that he'd come to be the founding member and leader of Killdoom, a band that could be described as a violent yet controlled surplus of the members themselves. *Killdoom*: "deliberately spoiling the hysterical doom of others through compassion or overly affected behaviour."

The visual series for the Alberta post-punk band's first EP evoked David Lynch's early short films: shot in black and white with flashes of stop-motion interspersed with figures navigating a haunted cube filled with junk. Killdoom's catalogue seemed to me a visual mood collage depicting the fringes of urban life. In this creepy video of theirs, the members of the band metalized themselves; body makeup made them into machines, into a virile gang.

On stage, Jack Chiang was powerful and scary, vibrating his hands or shaking his arms numb. He was an unruly thing with his acidic yelps and brainy, self-aware lyrics that seemed to intentionally avoid all possible pretension. A woman with a four-point leather harness over her naked breasts provided him with the necessary backup vocals as she ran about the floor in a circle of violence, moshing with the crowd.

Jack Chiang loved it.

The interviews that led up to what would be the first of many articles about Killdoom—articles appearing in *The Quietus, The Guardian, Loud and Quiet, Yin Yang Magazine, The List, Le Guess Who?, Medium, Birthday Cake for Breakfast, The Fader, Huck Mag, CVLTNation, Neon Waste, Untitled Magazine*—went from placing them as a Calgary band subscribing to the neo-Marxist school of post-punk to a Vancouver-via-Alberta multimedia collective and recovery program. The band's music was first reissued in the UK then in North America. Publicity that centred around both the interviews and the reissuing started in May 2016. Which was when they began to use their identity as a political weapon.

Now, in 2020, with Jack Chiang dead, the ghost of the band is unmistakable to fans: their dense videos and screen-printed outfits have the paramilitary chic of anarchist punk. It's an arresting spectacle, this seven-piece band with twenty or so members behind the scenes and growing.

As they toured Europe in early 2018, the band photographed every person they met and told fans to send their own face-shots. Face after face after face. Eventually, this stream of faces was incorporated, through Multi Face Blender, into one of the band's music videos—all those many faces became just one face. One face on the head of Jack Chiang.

I streamed a live performance from Paris, which was part of this two-year tour through Europe. In it, during what appeared to be a set-up rehearsal, Killdoom tested their equipment: the saxophone erupted in blurts and squiggles; cymbals crashed down over the room; bouncing, dub-indebted bass lines and skronking guitars were peppered throughout; there were droning atmospheres and a relentless motorik beat; pop-leaning afro-punk polyrhythms pushed a political agenda that antagonized power structures from a philosophical standpoint—power structures that had failed Jack Chiang's family when his father became sick and then died, leaving a single mother without an income and three children. How would I describe it? The vertigo of not knowing which direction is falling and which is up. Perhaps, I was only projecting my amazement and maybe envy at the death he had made for himself.

When I read his interview with *The Guardian* online, I realized Jack Chiang had said it best himself: "Artistic and punk communities initially seem inclusive and welcoming. But if you strip away the 'multicultural facades' from many DIY scenes, you're left with a lot of privilege. We didn't have that. We're not art students. We're coming from a different place." Despite the band's self-reflexivity, they had tokenized themselves: a tall Canadian-Pakistani man with a beard, dyed blond hair, and gold nail polish. Though Canadian-born, like Jack Chiang, he was needlessly framed as the son of immigrants.

Only two members were ever named: Jack Chiang and Muhammad. The rest of the musicians in the band were stand-ins who'd been paid off by Uncle Victor to tour through the UK and Europe with the band. They traveled the same circuit five times a year, performing their material, one appearance following the next. Each month became the next month, and in this way August became September. AUG 16 FR Saint-Malo, AUG 17 PL Gdansk, AUG 19 GE Berlin, AUG 20 GE Mainz, AUG 21 NL Utrecht, AUG 22 BE Liège, AUG 23 NL Rotterdam, AUG 24 FR Guéret, SEP 1 UK Larmer Tree Gardens, and so on and so forth, for as long as it took for his nephew and his nephew's friends to become famous.

This story is nothing new. What's strange is that they lied about Uncle Victor's financial involvement. The entire band left him out of the narrative. I could taste the sour grapes of their lie in everything they stood for.

The Guardian interview ended with an admission: "If people think we look like a cult, then we're making our mark." I wouldn't have called them marked. But, then again, I don't really know how marked people behave. Supposedly, shortly before the incident, some of the more anonymous members of the band threatened to leave and form their own group.

Jack Chiang's real life contradicted everything. Killdoom's love-everyone tyranny was still about anger and drugs and sex. The uselessness of his art was really just the equivocal intrigue of our own personal truths. Through this intrigue, he ground the memories of his father to nothing. To empty potential. It was clear to me that becoming famous as Jack Chiang had become famous was the most cowardly act.

Ichi-go ichi-e

If you meet a Buddha, kill him; if you meet a patriarch, kill him; if you meet a sage, kill him; if you meet your father or mother, kill them; if you meet your relatives, kill them. Only then will you obtain liberation and dwell in complete emancipated freedom, without getting emotionally caught up in things. – Rinzai

Shouldering the divine simulacrum, the mikoshi men chanted "*Wasshoi wasshoi!*" and passed slowly through the large torii into the cemetery's temporary shrine. But Takao Abe was not feeling particularly festive. He felt abysmal. Perhaps because the weather was so abysmal. He had no idea why the tourists were looking at him so much. All those innumerable, reeking Western tourists, who had drunk their innumerable, reeking beers in Sapporo and were now missing the mikoshi's radiant beauty. He would be only too happy to knock them all down, this noisy group, to smash all the curious figures into many pieces with one single blow of his fist.

Their spying presence filled him with disgust. They never ceased with their vulgar spying. They constantly badgered him with insinuations. If someone from this group dared to ask him about the death of his brother—someone who didn't speak Japanese and would likely mispronounce *hara-kiri*, saying instead "hiri-kiri" or even "hari-kari"—he wouldn't hesitate to strike them dead without a word. He'd end the life of anyone who gave the slightest hint of anything like an approach toward the gruesome topic of seppuku.

He passed under the great torii and walked along the entranceway for a short distance before turning onto a path that wound around the outside of the cemetery. Another short distance later, he turned onto an even narrower path, which led into the cemetery. From here, he made his way directly past the masses of stonework and small memorials where sprigs of star anise grew, to the attraction with which his client had charged Takao Abe & Associates, his architecture firm. This client wanted his firm to give visitors of their cemetery a more serene appreciation of the Buddha. The cemetery comprised many hectares of lush land and gently sloping hills of black pine, but the Daibutsu sat alone in a field, unsheltered from the weather.

Everything about this Buddha, from its rounded shoulders to the folds of its robe, was on a grand scale. Its chest was partially visible, protruding from the graceful lines of the sleeves that flowed down from its shoulders. Snails coiled like hair on the Buddha's head, its long earlobes hung like dried fruit from a tropical tree, and its eyes were sick with bloom.

But the cold stone had nothing to say of the Buddha.

Takao Abe turned his gaze away from the Daibutsu onto the emptiness, onto the unbuilt-ness, onto the pure possibility. He then closed his eyes and let himself see the stretch of cemetery beyond the graves. And like Minerva, born from the forehead of Jupiter, he comprehended the situation with wisdom: the project would be on the scale of landscape rather than architecture. Which meant that it was going to be a challenge—for all his ideas and designs typically culminated in building his own masterworks, not in enhancing those of another builder. Always one step ahead, he was already dealing with his reaction to that consideration. Already he was telling himself, *I have to go forward. You have to go forward. Otherwise you lose. Go on living. Go on working.*

The rain wasn't falling as hard as it had been that morning. The pavement, covered with moss and fallen leaves, glistened in the winter shower. Takao Abe was without rain gear and was dressed in an old Western-style suit. His bulging necktie was fastened around his sweat-stained collar, and his face had taken on the hard and sombre expression of an insect. Despite his discomfort, he wanted to walk awhile to collect his thoughts.

Creation was fighting. Designing was a battle. When he was nineteen years old, following in the footsteps of his older brother, he'd fought a dozen professional kendo matches. And in his spare time, he'd visited not only Buddhist temples throughout Japan, the designs of which fascinated him beyond all expectation, but also Daibutsu statues, which were inevitably there too. So he wasn't completely unfamiliar with the Japanese tradition of giant Buddha statues. He knew, for instance, that historically, the Daibutsu were made of wood, then bronze. Now, apparently, they were made of stone. He recalled the renowned works of colossal statuary and then considered this particular big Buddha, beginning to formulate what the completed project would look like. There was more than enough time for that. Time wasn't a problem. There was no reason to hurry.

As he watched the statue, fascination gradually overtook him. Little by little, he edged closer to it. At length he looked and examined, and as he probed up and around the Buddha, it seemed that he was and was not. He felt his existence and did not feel it. He felt that all this before him might vanish, and that he too might vanish. Just one sunya thing evanescing into another. At that moment, all the statue's surroundings were there only to serve it. It was the very hub, the very nucleus of the universe.

I'm going to have to rearrange the environment, Takao Abe thought, on the high-speed train headed back to Osaka. He would have to shape the landscape around the preexisting statue. It was a landscape project and nothing else—exclusively a landscape project, even if there was a figure of the Buddha involved. He couldn't repeat this often enough to himself. But for now, he didn't say anything, either to himself or out loud. For several kilometres he simply sketched in silence. Because why say anything? No one understood, anyway. Better to be quiet and sketch.

After several solitary hours had passed, Takao Abe found himself quite hungry, so he went to the train's sushi restaurant, sat at the bar, and ordered a sukiyaki dinner. No one else was around. The cook chipped at the crusted ash in the cold hibachi with a pair of tongs and then, after putting on a fresh apron, threw himself into the task of chopping vegetables. His busy fingertips filled platters with multi-coloured sashimi and broiled fish and meats.

Lying there in the lamplight, Takao Abe's plate of sushi seemed dull and pale. As he ate, he tried to think about how best to deal with the project, but chewing interfered with his calculations. He acknowledged that the silence of eating sushi was a relief to him. After all, how many more times before he died, he wondered, would he experience the pleasure of eating?

Whenever Takao Abe talked about his brother's suicide, he could either describe it but not be able to explain it, or he could explain it but not be able to describe it. But really, he didn't need words to make himself understood. He always understood it best when he operated in silence. Given that he had the mind of a twenty-first-century-ite, he struggled to express his thoughts on the topic. For seppuku was an idea that did not belong to this era—it was an intolerable idea of beauty and purity that stubbornly refused to be acknowledged as what it truly was: not only pure righteousness but also pure evil.

The Daibutsu was a grievous sight: a Daibutsu that had lost its world. So enormous, immeasurably enormous—and yet it was nothing at all. It didn't belong here nor anywhere upon the earth, having originated from a heavenly realm beyond concept that no longer existed because the heavenly realm of Vajrayana, of the truly eternal present, had itself disappeared from the human world.

Takao Abe wondered when and why something like a Buddha would come to this world. It was difficult to encounter a Buddha. He seemed to remember reading somewhere that you would meet one only once in a million kalpas. *At first,* he thought, *we look for support from the person closest to us—not a Buddha. But clinging to this person ultimately means the suicide of our spirit, the suicide of our being, our soul. Then we think that we must turn to the professionals of the mind, the soul, the world of things. But in them we meet only deep disappointment.* It was obvious to Takao Abe that no help was to be expected from anywhere at all, and under no circumstances from people living the religious life.

And yet it remained here, this Daibutsu from a heavenly realm remained in the region where Takao Abe's samurai ancestors had once guarded and pacified the Jomon people of northern Honshū and Hokkaidō, until Abe no Sadato surrendered. After which, Abe no Sadato's adversaries returned to Kyoto, carrying his head.

Takao Abe's brother had had a Shinto wedding and a Buddhist funeral. His body had been arranged in the zazen position inside the sitting coffin, giving the appearance that he was a warrior in silent meditation. After that, Takao Abe had started taking a route past an old temple whenever he cycled home from work at the Osaka office. The doors were always open. He'd been meaning to go in, just to see what it looked like inside. He wondered why he hadn't—why he hadn't gone inside and sat down for the evening chants and silent group meditation and then listened to the temple's quiet. Maybe it was insecurity. Maybe awkwardness. Maybe just laziness.

The answer to the design problem, when it finally came, was an evasion. Though in danger of losing the forest for the trees, Takao Abe nonetheless reasoned that if he were to conceal the religious artifact within the very land itself, the Daibutsu would no longer need to be on display. In fact, it would no longer be a Daibutsu but a hibutsu, a hidden Buddha. It wouldn't be available for regular viewing, but it would still draw crowds of thousands during specific public events, such as kaichō ceremonies. This evasive solution he'd been searching for came during an afternoon in the office, when he was bent over a meaningless architectural blueprint. If Takao Abe really was a genius and the world of his architecture mere emptiness, then why shouldn't he be able to prove it? As an architect, he was at the centre of society. He had planned and planned and planned many of the world's masterful works.

The many drawings rose up beneath his hands. There were no beginnings or ends to them, just moments of continuation. And everything—the spirit, the people, and the geography—all met in one genius loci: the figure of the Buddha. And because all Buddhists believed that the Buddha represented reality, Takao Abe wasn't quite sure what to call his idea. *Cognitively, the Buddha is dead,* he thought, *but affectively, he is alive.* This idea clung to his mind like rust, and he felt a black satisfaction in not naming it. Suddenly, he no longer felt human. That is to say, without ceasing to be a human being, he came into another mode of being in which he got rid of the human part of himself—a part of himself that was merely a thing to all other beings. A dead object. And he became obsessed with something in the part of himself that he had exiled. There was something sinister, something ominous about it. At that moment, he was certain that he was holding the seeds of a problem immense enough to fill the vast emptiness of the cosmos.

His brother had purchased a short blade called a tantō. He'd worn a white cotton kimono and matching *hakama,* a costume worn for death. The white clothing had seemed to enhance his brother's air of quiet determination. These culturally significant objects led Takao Abe to speculate about what style of self-disembowelment his brother had eventually chosen. Perhaps single-line disembowelment (*ichimonji-bara*) or crosswise disembowelment (*jumonji-bara*)? Maybe crosswise disembowelment in modified T-shape (*henkei jumonji-bara*)? Or even vertical disembowelment (*nambu-bara*)? He couldn't remember which.

Takao Abe's brother had requested that he be the *kaishakunin* in the ritual suicide. "I cannot commit hara-kiri alone," his brother had said. Because after he sliced open his stomach, his intestines would spill onto a small metal tray, and then, having severed the descending aorta, he was sure to die of blood loss or shock if Takao Abe did not decapitate him.

It would be an act of loyalty without courage—an act shot through with anger and burning, with emotional contempt. It would be loyalty that was almost betrayal.

The only way Takao Abe could cope with contempt of this sort was to hold onto a belief in his own nobility, and this he did with moderation rather than with the blind traditionalism of his brother. To be the kaishakunin, however, was to take part in a detailed ritual, as Takao Abe's laidō classes would reveal. He remembered his conundrum well.

To perform kaishaku *will mean destroying my brother at the moment of his final agony. It's all directed against my brother, everything I've ever done in my life, perhaps. Instinctively, I've always acted against my brother. And now, by realizing my role as* kaishakunin *in the ritual of* kaishaku, *I am proceeding most radically against my brother. These proceedings are proceedings against my brother.*

The courage that had then propelled Takao Abe to learn how to perform the task of kaishaku had frightened him: his hands had trembled. To calm his nerves, he'd visualized himself as a Japanese Zen monk in the kyudojo releasing the arrow from his bow toward a target. His passion had all the semblance of fire with no function of burning.

Takao Abe would build a prayer hall to enhance the attractiveness of the stone Buddha sculpted so many years ago, by some anonymous sculptor. He'd even gone so far as to inquire with various bureaus about the statue's biography, but he'd received no results. He felt a tense indecisiveness. The movements and gestures that would lead him to complete his project were not the movements and gestures of faith and devotion to his craft but those of fear and hope—fear and hope that somehow it would become visible that nothing he did was true, sincere, open, or natural.

It was he, right here in his office in Osaka, who surmounted everything with the greatest of sensitivity, because he alone had a heart he could feel, and with his heart he looked at the landscape project. He could see it now, too. Even though Takao Abe was no longer in its presence, the Daibutsu was still deep in his mind, and it was with his heart that he could now see that everything was woven into one undivided essence—for the kami, derived from nature, would always be present: the kami of the earth with the kami of the water, the kami of the water with the kami of the sky, the kami of the wind, the kami of the sea and river, the kami of thunder, flowers, rocks, forests, even the kami of the human. Because into the earth and the water and the sky, into this indescribable cosmos, was woven humankind's fragile existence as well—but merely just one moment that could not be traced. For as soon as it appeared it was no more. It disappeared for all eternity, irrevocably. Nothing else remained.

Only and exclusively the landscape project on Takao Abe's drafting table.

Everything was there in his hand and his heart. He measured precisely, looking at the drawing plans continuously, to measure accurately and to draw accurately. His brother's repeated clapping in reverence to the gods before committing seppuku still echoed through him.

After Takao Abe had set out food and drink, he drank a farewell cup of sake with his brother, who sat down facing east upon a tatami mat and unfastened his kimono. His brother ate very little, believing it unseemly to have food pour out when the sword cut into his stomach. Takao Abe brushed his brother's cheeks lightly with rouge, so that the glow of health might remain even after his death. Then his brother took up his short sword, cut open his stomach with it, and pressed his blade to his throat in gesture.

"This is the correct place, brother. Strike with graceful dispatch and bring my life to a brave conclusion."

Thus, having been issued the order to strike off his brother's head, Takao Abe—filled with grief at such a parting, having no will to strike such a blow—converted his sadness to anger.

He unsheathed his sword, lifted it above his head, and took aim at his brother's neck. In an instant, Takao Abe's blade came sweeping down. And then the corpse slumped forward in fulfillment of the ritual.

His brother, who'd felt oppressed by his sense of responsibility, had begun preparing to take his own life after his own company, Abe Construction, suffered financial losses. He'd written a short death poem, no more than a line, upon the white headband—now flecked with fresh blood—that he'd worn the night of his last kendo match: "With death, all is purified."

Takao Abe took the headband off the severed head to read the poem and then hurriedly screwed it up into a ball and threw it to the floor. He couldn't help feeling that a thrill of joy had gone through him with the knife. His clear voice had been like a blade cutting through his brother's core shame.

"*Ichi-go ichi-e*, brother."

Death in Absentia

Baptiste Picq made the sign of the cross over the omen. It seemed to be the usual practice, either to ward off some threat the omen might pose or to give it one's blessing. In this case, it was no doubt the latter.

I have a desire to be anywhere, he thought. *Anywhere out of this world. Or at least out of this place.*

The birds never rested here, yet for all their activity, they found only the rare worm. In the setting sun, an eagle-owl had become stunned by the many multi-coloured rays as soon as it rose into the air. And when the eagle-owl fell, though nobody was there to see it, Baptiste Picq heard the dull thud in the distance. Despite the bloody fall, its wings beat wildly. A flurry of feathered claws folded and turned, turned and folded. Now, the omen lay on the ground. Motionless. The bird no longer a bird.

Despite his insistence on godlessness, Baptiste Picq was always on the lookout for just such signs and symbols. He stared at the eagle-owl's monstrous eyes.

Nearby, a pair of red-haired cecropia moths mated near the eagle-owl with such ineffable softness that Baptiste Picq's own body trembled at the sight of their insect desires, trembled at the sight of love and death, joined.

Then, suddenly, he crushed them into pulp between his toes. From the huge, mangled stain on his foot, long, wispy antennae grasped for signs of their own life.

*

Baptiste Picq smelled of wine fumes.

He had a feeling of acedia toward his duties here—here being the cresset from which the incense of religion burned: the monastery. The abbey was home to some sixty cenobite monks who lived by the motto "pray and work," manual labour being the abbey's mainstay—enough labour for a passerby to believe that the slothful monks were hard at work.

The alcoholic's trembling hand poured wine from the copper vat, a vat full of minimally fermented mustum. Without alcohol, the pure grape wine was now only half as sacred as before, and after drinking copious amounts of it, Baptiste Picq felt more bloated and sober than ever.

He was starting to believe that he'd contracted the habit of drunkenness because of that Noonday Demon, the Meridian Demon, specifically responsible for acedia and the disease of drink. The demon attacked the cenobite monks most frequently between the hours of ten and two. This demonic figure, active as it was in the noon hours, inclined its victims to listlessness, restlessness, torpor, ennui, boredom, and depression.

When Baptiste Picq made his way through the wine and decanted it into his brain, his rage became almost immeasurable, and he'd lash out indiscriminately, at everything in sight. In the face of his brothers' reproaches, he'd reformed temporarily and adopted a more taciturn disposition. Nobody had been able to get near him then, though. And now, he seethed with a secret resentment at this notion of duty, which prevented him from resolving the guilt that had piled up within him like a mountain of moose antlers.

While staying at the abbey, Baptiste Picq didn't contemplate the ruin of human beings. At least not enough to work out his thoughts on the subject. His gaze, though gentle, was deep enough to know that human destiny had no connection with the stars.

Red, sweaty, Baptiste Picq was afraid. Afraid because he knew he had another being inside him. Like a moth ecloses after pupation, he too was plummeting from his lost body, from its disintegrated elements, after the final moult.

After a tiring night of drinking the mustum, having gained a momentary psychological advantage over his boredom, he crossed rapidly through the long rows of abandoned and silent rooms with their paneling and wainscoting, their mirrors and curtains. Then he slept in the leaden vaults that ran along the foundations of the ancient monastery.

*

Baptiste Picq started every day with a canonical cup of coffee and some cheese. The practice was true folly, deprecated by all the other cenobite monks in the abbey. Every morning starting at four-fifty A.M., clad in their habiliments, the priestly caste of cenobite monks knelt in prayer for two hours before the crucifix at the centre of the church's sanctuary altar or, if they preferred, in their own cells. Their devotion never concluded.

Baptiste Picq was sitting on a bench in a clearing at the top of a hill. Overlooking a lake, he would drink his coffee and eat his cheese by means of an almost imperceptible bite, noticing, as he did so, the veins creeping along the surface of the piece of blue cheese wrapped in greasy, cylindrical wax paper.

He made a hole in the earth with a piece of pointed wood and then filled his palm with soil. Baptiste Picq brought this sustenance, the earth, to his mouth as if it were a palate cleanser between pieces of cheese, and then flung it quickly away without ingesting it.

Now that the ruins of autumn had arrived, the great comestibles fair was on its way—that cheesy fair, the Winter Fair in Toronto, which took place from the first of November to the tenth. During this time, Baptiste Picq would, in full canonical wear, take the monks' assorted cheeses to other markets, world markets, and to other fairs, world fairs, unbeknownst to the cloisters of toad-faced brothers, who only ever took the cheese to the Winter Fair and not a fair farther. Because this year, he'd decided, they were going to get the big financial push they needed.

From the bench, the abbey looked as much like a medieval castle as it did a centre for religious devotion. Farther afield lay an apple orchard. A bell tower at the building's centre stretched into the sky, high above the dome of the cathedral, and when the bells rang, the sound echoed up and up, toward the serene regions of the good.

The monastery had been founded by Benedictine monks who'd been driven from France by anti-clerical laws. Baptiste Picq himself was now a Catholic—a Catholic who'd been baptized after his sixtieth year. He hadn't been heard from, or at least Franciscus Picq hadn't been heard from, for almost seven years. And so the court was about to declare Franciscus Picq legally dead, a judicial determination in the absence of his body. There were no clear indicia of death: no rigor mortis or decomposition, no lack of brain or cardiac activity, no traumatic injury incompatible with life. Franciscus Picq was merely presumed to be dead. He was dead in absentia.

Trial in absentia might have worked if they were in Italy, but this was Canada, and in Canada, "it's the defendant's right to be present in the court proceedings of his criminal trial," his defence attorney had told him almost seven years ago. So he'd been placed at the abbey, driven, in a sense, from convict to convent, so as to be out of the public eye as much as possible. He'd been a COO for five years, but as a result of an unofficial vote, he'd been asked to step down for the sake of the company's other executive members. His defence attorney had told him: "Try, just try, to make an effort at the abbey until things die down, blow over. Avoid scandals. Let other companies take the hit."

He was going to die. And Franciscus Picq would have to remain dead for the rest of his life. Those were the rules. He'd never be present to answer the charges. At the abbey, he had freedom of religion but not freedom from religion. He worshiped only the coffer in his wardrobe drawer, and there was no longer much money to be made. First the scandal and then his drinking— God would be a triple crime for him, for he would never keep faith.

Baptiste Picq could often hear the echoes of Gregorian chants drawing visitors into the chapel, down the hallway lined with paintings of triptychs and Madonnas, to where a dozen cenobite monks took part in prayer. The cenobite monks spent most of their days in silence and followed a strict schedule: prayer, scripture reading, and meditation. Today, Baptiste Picq had shirked the schedule. He hadn't prayed, he hadn't read scripture, and he hadn't meditated. Nothing at all.

Life is just one long prayer anyway.

Instead, Baptiste Picq was foraging in the woods. He needed fresh ingredients for the batch of cheese he was presently at work on for the fair. The cheese was going to be his way out. The other cenobite monks had noticed the break in Baptiste Picq's routine, his obvious drinking problem, and the skipping out on his official cardinal duties and working the business side of things "with blasphemous eagerness." He heard their mutterings and plots against him before they plunged once more into their self-absorbed orisons, like tortoises into their shells.

The cheese factory was closed to the public, which was why Baptiste Picq liked it. Downstairs, in the padlocked cupboards of the ripening room, was where the cheese was stored. It was in this crypt in the cathedral that he made his blue cheese: a hard, blue-veined cheese with hints of roqueforti mushrooms.

As he foraged, a huge yawn wandered Baptiste Picq's throat. He finally liberated it after several hours, this generous yawn, and right away shielded it with his hand. *What is religion?* He hadn't given much thought to it. Like all books, the Bible had been written by human beings. And with God buried and Satan dead, well, what more was there for a monk to do? To do as the Buddha did? To do as Christ did? *No, it serves us right for choosing a god in our own image—an image we can be damned by.* He didn't know the difference between good and evil, and the Crucified One didn't answer his questions. Chance had been kind to him. To him, his path was not sacred.

*

I would take nothing with me because I don't need anything from here.

Baptiste Picq tried the next wood. It was too late for soft berries, but he thought there might be apples and maybe some woodland mushrooms. *There'll definitely be hazelnuts by now.* He knew where to look for them.

He began to walk, on padding, naked feet, down the hill toward the foraging place. He'd left behind his heavy, tattered leather sandals, had placed them neatly under the bench so that the skin of his feet could fully take on the characteristics of all ten billion bacteria cells living in the rhizosphere: actinomycetes, fungi, algae, and protozoa—soil microorganisms in and around plant roots that were now making their way under his miraculous toenails, toenails which he'd let grow for a fortnight.

He came upon an apple tree and shook the branches before skipping around with his basket to gather the fallen fruit. *We do eat a lot of fruits and vegetables,* he thought. *Must have been such a relief when one of the monks invented cheese.* The cenobite monks had time to make cheese, and to have rituals and festivals. *People just need time. With time, they can decide to make something real through work.*

Baptiste Picq really wanted to find those mushrooms. He'd seen them growing in the woods the other day. On the way, he ate a couple of wild hazelnuts green, right off the tree, while shouldering the brimming bag he'd already filled with nuts. He eventually came to a thicket before heading uphill.

The monastery was approximately half an hour away when Baptiste Picq noticed, with alarm that was sudden but belated, that he was lost. And no wonder. He was within a municipality unto itself, a kind of Vatican City in miniature.

His face, an amen face, an august face, had taken on the pallor of cheese and the features of a criminal. Strands of hair had fallen over his forehead and were curling like fresh salad. Storm clouds crossed the sky, and it started raining. All life around him became drenched and morphed into uglier and unfamiliar versions of itself. It was a miracle that he found the mushrooms. *All miracles are a sign of God's laziness,* he thought.

It was already late afternoon: the hour of the cheese. In a moment of relief, Baptiste Picq heard the almost imperceptible trembling, a rumbling of heavy benediction, of the bell, that signal for the bee-like cenobite monks going about their holy toil. Water rose at the back of his square mouth. He knew which way to go now, and he felt as though he could die of hunger on the spot.

*

There really isn't any rush, but I don't like debts. I like to settle them—to be done with them.

Baptiste Picq looked at those various mushy, specially cultured bacteria, the cheese-pale faces of the roqueforti fungus variety. He looked at the cheeses, so delicately lined with veins and spotted throughout with blue, blue-grey, and blue-green mould. He sniffed, voluntarily, expertly, the distinct odours of ripened milk and mould, of cow's milk, sheep's milk, goat's milk, and water buffalo's milk cheeses, in the cool dampness. The bacterium *Brevibacterium linens,* responsible as it was for the smell of many blue cheeses, as well as for his own foot odour, was aged in a temperature-controlled environment such as this cave-like ripening room, which gave it that sense of penicillium freedom.

The cenobite monks hadn't called him Baptiste "Piquant" Picq for nothing. It seemed to them that the thrust of inspiration ran through him at times, as if he'd rediscovered the Roquefort shepherds' secret alchemy of milk, bread, air, and time all over again. For a non-Christian heart, the inspiration would have been another. But for Baptiste Picq, who'd been part of the C-suite, a Bay-street guru before the financial crisis ran him out, a more cost-effective variation on the Roquefort-style cheese was sure to be enough to keep him feverishly busy.

Baptiste Picq was so fascinated by his nauseating occupation that nothing else seemed to exist for him. Studying his clever variations with a thudding heart, he'd feel as delighted as if he were already at the festival. But the time had come to draw in the reins of that inspiration and to stop for a moment along the way, as when he used to look at women's vaginas. For he knew the cenobite monks sensed that something was happening here, that something special was a-brew, that something, though nothing obvious, was going to happen, and so they were observing everything about him, patiently, ready to see what the future would bring.

The milk had already become solid through acidification, so he cut the thick curds with the gentle blade of a knife to release the whey, salted them to taste, and then gave the cheese its form by pressing it with weights. The final step was to ripen the cheese by aging it. After the aged curds had been pierced, air tunnels would form in the cheese, and veins would lead the mould around in the pressed form. When given oxygen, the mould could grow, could feed, along the surface of the curd-air interface, and blue streaks would form throughout. A breathing corpse.

There had been three kings of blue cheese over the decades: Roquefort in 1070, from France, Gorgonzola in 1707, from Italy, and Stilton in 1722, from England. Baptiste Picq didn't want to invent yet another blue cheese. He wanted to attain something that everyone could understand was different. He wanted a regional product. One that would bear his own abbey's name and protect its reputation geographically, so that only the cenobite monks would ever be allowed to manufacture, process, and prepare the cheese—here, at the abbey, in the vilifying origin of the thing.

Although penicillium could be found naturally, modern cheese producers tended to use commercially manufactured penicillium cultures that had been freeze-dried. Baptiste Picq had trod over the woodlands, on apples and hazelnuts, on mushrooms and soil, with the physical instrument of his toes, those charmed joints between which the mould grew—soon to be freeze-dried. He'd injected some of the cheese with spores from this inimitable big toe before the curds formed. In others, he'd mixed the spores with the curds after they'd formed.

Cheese by cheese, Baptiste Picq prepared the award-winning stock for the fair's vendor. Face serious, wrinkled toward thoughts of commerce, and with the invitation to the Winter Fair in his sacrilegious hands, Baptiste Picq huddled with the uncertain attitudes adopted by the somewhat cross-looking faces of that consternate cheese.

Like God, the cheese gave no sapient reply. He thought and thought about his question, about the purpose of his waiting in absentia at the abbey, the question of whether there was any purpose in doing so, any person meant to appear. If that person didn't come, there would be no one and nothing to answer him.

The answer wasn't coming. He'd have to leave with no answer. Move on to the next question.

Cathedral of Spiders

My body hangs suspended from a cross.

It can't fall. It can't get off the cross. It wants to free itself from the cross. It wants to fall below, far lower than before, to the next point in lowness. But no future point is ever low enough. And at no point will it ever stop falling. Because at every lower point, it wants the points still further below it, and those lower points attract it more and more. It's drawn by a dark tendency to what's lower, and its fall remains an infinite descent. Downward. Toward the bottom. Toward an end obscured by limitless darkness. If at some point it finishes falling, it will end its existence. It will no longer be what it is: my body. It will not continue: it will cease to be life.

To release myself from this cross, toward the uncrucified world above, I must change. From this moment on, all must change, everything must change, nothing must last the gestation period. I must grow wings and rise on the new earth, under a new sky. There's no other way but up. Not upward, but in a direction without a name. Not toward the past or the future but in a direction away from the planet of time.

An unreal, eternal ascension: an inconceivable turn, inside out.

What dies on the cross isn't me. For a brief moment, it's God who dies and passes through the abyss of atheism.

This isn't a story. Neither is it a spell, a gift, or a curse. It's an exit plan, a forward escape into the imagination. What's been written so far belongs to the forbidden files of my dossier, but there's nothing especially occult or esoteric about it. To convince myself that these raw materials are really there, I speculatively reread, reconstruct, relive them each day.

The text itself has some gaps. Some lines are crossed out, some overlap. It breathes uneasiness, uncertainty, bewilderment. For years I have altered it, rearranged it, excogitating variants, mentally omitting one letter or writing one letter too many, and yet the text remains unfinished. It should be torn up. Sometimes I feel like throwing it against the wall. But I'm addicted, corrupted, converted. And like God, I'm always either soliloquizing my mistakes or dramatizing my errors. Deep inside my fictionlust, I may imagine I loathe and love these mistakes and errors that I've constructed, or feel something for them, but according to the purpose of my narrative desires, I'm utterly deceiving myself.

I'm afraid to begin this story, a story with no definite end. There's no single structure I can name here, no crystalized normality around which I can base the experience of my life, nothing that I can't doubt any more than I can doubt the very room where I'm writing this now, a room in a city in a postanthropic culture on a planet in space. On an old bed, I lie down passively, supine, in a kind of resignation, and wait for the end. I don't sleep. I've never truly slept because I know that the moment I close my eyes, my senses will shut down and I'll be defenceless, giving myself to the monstrously enormous world, without protection. Renouncing things like sleep is less difficult than people believe. It's a matter of getting started. And once you've succeeded in dispensing with something you thought essential, you realize you can also do without something else, then without many other things.

I have the feeling, as I often do when I close the door behind me and find myself writing in an isolated place, that everyone outside has disappeared, forever, and that I'm locked inside, forever. Alone, always alone, more alone than the last person on Earth. I feel that entities as different from me as I am from a cloud or lake are, in a way that I can't comprehend, observing me.

I'm made to catalogue and sort everything, every word I've ever written, according to the logic of grotesque, hallucinogenic nightmares and old memories. I want to reread my story and cry again, just to be shut inside the body and mind of someone who disappeared from this world so many years ago. The past, engrammed in my archaic memory loops, neither fully fades nor becomes inaccessible. Sickeningly remembered images from my childhood and my adolescence flash through my mind.

Feeling how unreal the room and the world are, I walk to the window and look absently at the scene outside, at the vast and melancholy landscape of the end. Maybe I'm dreaming, although I'm here, and everything can be touched, smelled, and seen without the possibility of doubt.

Within the crumbling walls of the second storey of an old chapel, I still live. I live psychedelically, in a weirder experience, in an atmosphere of continuous unfolding and understanding. Every day I know more, see into things with greater depth than I did before. This will be my last home. I've lived here for many years now in complete solitude. I wouldn't even recognize the other members of my own species if I happened upon Them, as though out of nowhere I might run into creatures who resembled me in every way. I'm alive, but only as another animal in a natural place, a creature among other creatures.

I eat a miserable supper by the light of funeral candles and the frightening, fungal stars of a strange zodiac. Then I sit in deep contemplation of the thin fishbones and the remnants of an unknown species of dried, psilocybin-containing mushroom, long after the actual content—a truly alien compound produced by many species of plants and animals, and causing dramatically different psychedelic states, impossible feelings, and unimaginable behaviours and magical experiences—has been consumed by the acids of my stomach.

Everything on the plate must be eaten, I tell myself every day of my life, no matter how disgusting or how difficult to swallow it might be. I eat with little to no pleasure, almost unconsciously. Once a bite is in my mouth, I chew once or twice, and then there seems to be no other choice, at that point, but to swallow. I vomit, I start over, I vomit again. As I eat, tears drip. A cistern of tears. I'm crying and I'm writing and I'm nibbling absentmindedly while believing, as I do most days, due to my reconfigured senses on psilocybin, that I'm an alien occupying a human body. I sometimes interpret myself as an entity stealing the shape of another being. I remind myself, again and again, that I've always been this human body.

Yet I nonetheless begin to feel as if I'm an alien experiencing the life of a human named Brandon Teigland. I seem to have my own life elsewhere but am currently reading and writing the higher-dimensional story of Brandon Teigland. Once Brandon Teigland dies, I'll return to my real life. I can even sense my life will end with a release into a higher-dimensional place. And I feel eager yet patient to return to my world. I think about this often without dread or despair. Because all I know now is Brandon Teigland, but soon I'll complete my job and return to my life. I sense maybe I'm here to gather information. To collect data on humans.

My task is terrible, total, universal, and merciless. I've made myself a character in my own story. A fictitious character. A character I've invented. A higher-dimensional character in a story who's writing a story. I describe endlessly, page after page, a plot empty of people but full of myself. I always try to write about my life in this or that way, and I never write about anything but death because literature has the same relationship to life as life has to death.

I don't want to write anymore. I don't even want to write anything about myself, about the vanished world. I'm merely attempting to understand my life by facing the ultimate meaning to which all stories refer and all plots tend to move toward: the continuation of life and the inevitability of death.

I won't write anything because the moment I write anything, I'm overwhelmed with my manuscript, this ugly document, an apocalyptic realist's auto-crucifixion, a blackened dystopian vignette of opulent desolation and baroque monstrosity, the one to which I'm now adding phrases such as "Ideas exist. Curious ideas, fascinating ideas, obsessive ideas, maniacal ideas. They are never our own. They are the consequences of a desire—a desire that does not yet exist, but which, since we want it to exist, cannot fail to exist."

Suddenly there's a shimmering. I blow out the candles, and within seconds, in total darkness, I'm in another realm, astonished. Some part of me eats the final bite of my meal and I relax into another place. I sense I'm in the presence of a faceless, bodiless, genderless abstraction, and the experience feels almost like sex, very erotic. It's an intensely sexual and relational symbiosis with the spirit of another species. A relationship that I ingest in a range of doses to determine if it's toxic or not.

The marrow of a strange, warm fear flows inside my bones with a dull roar, like a waterfall, and my long black fingernails leave bloody tattoos on my skin, evoking the white and lumpy worms of scarification. The mother of all terrors, the greatest of all horrors, is born for me, created for me. Dread deforms everything around me, drives me into a dark veil of indeterminacy, into a feeling of annihilation and paralysis before the absolutely clear atrocity of an eternity in which I no longer exist.

Am I the only survivor? Was it a few seconds ago that everything ceased to exist, or many centuries? The events that led to human demise undoubtedly happened to me, but I've already lost any sense of time. I want to believe that I exist but I can't. And while I may know humans don't exist, I don't know if I exist. I've never known it, I lack that knowledge, but I know it in the way that a person suffering from insomnia knows sleep, or a person watching the darkness knows light.

Yet I survived, the last human alive, infinitely isolated. It isn't clear how, and the deferment of my own disappearance doesn't seem to tell me much of anything about what I've survived. This enigma itself is a sign that I don't know and can't know anything about it. I often forget to think about my fate on Earth and about finding out what's happened. The thought occasionally comes into my mind and never leaves. The thought of an event that I've not yet decided to tell myself fully. I know what it is, at least in part. I know in fact what I think it is. But what terrifies me is what it possibly is.

I remember everything, although I can't imagine or describe it yet. I can't write about it here or now. I feel I know this information, but I can't just start writing about my transformation into the Other, into a new creature—my metamorphosis into an identical yet completely different being. I know I should be doing some serious thinking about these things, but I have no idea how to go about it. I don't know enough to worry. And honestly, thinking is the last thing I want to do. Because the time will come soon enough when I have no choice in the matter, and when that time comes, I'll take a good long time to think things over. Not now, though. Not now.

But if not now, when? I'll soon disappear, and once I disappear, there will be no one left. Because there is only one of me. I'm all there is.

I stand up, look out the window at the black, endless forest, pull the drapes shut, and then return to my desk and write again. Languaging experience: this is how I get out of my life. The walls are tattooed with minuscule letters, maniacal lines that begin legibly on the ceiling and end in scribbles on the mirror; stories are scrawled over clothing, inked on the sheets of the bed. I wrote all of it. Everything. In fact, as I consciously, subconsciously, and unconsciously wrote each and every letter, a disorienting and frightening feeling came over me.

I suddenly reconstruct something. My motion seems extradimensionally controlled, as if I'm inside a video game, which makes me feel as if I'm within the visual field of the eyes of a strange, unknown being. Something looking inside my body. I can feel its gaze in a higher dimension. It can see things it should never see. It can penetrate my mind, delve into the forbidden chamber of my brain, and examine the formation of my thoughts. I feel the weight of its gaze as it understands me. Not only wholly, from within and without and in seemingly all directions at once, but also stretched out in time, beginning with conception and ending with my decomposition, understanding in a glance not only the shape of my body and my fate but also the fate of the human species. It views everything, including me, within a context spanning the universe, from the formation of the sun in the Milky Way galaxy to the emergence of biology and its development on Earth, from microorganisms to fish to amphibians to reptiles to mammals to primates to Homo sapiens to a brief transformation called human history.

The end of history is feelable. It feels like being poisoned, like something's wrong. The older I am, the more I feel it, but it's a feeling that all living things, everything alive and nearing the end of time, must closely share.

I've been chosen. I'm the one chosen from billions like me, a kind of uncrowned prince, because all those who have ever lived have perished; all who began this journey have been devoured. A hundred billion humans metabolized by the universe, one by one. Or They died, all at once, in who knows what terrifying cataclysm. I'm the last one. I've somehow been spared the catastrophe that destroyed everyone else. The sheer boredom of this catastrophe gets to me. I try to ward off thoughts of what's to come. The end is coming, or an end. An end, at least, of some kind. But I can't think or write about it. Not another line anyways. Because the very thought of what's to come grips my stomach like a claw. The one thought that now, as I write, I see. I feel, I foretell, and I prophesy the merciless destruction that will come, that has come.

I remember it all, almost all of it, because of a flower. The plant, sent from some intervening God for me, blooms for me. The sensitive species grows only where I live, at the edge of my spiritual garden, in filtered-light-speckled seclusion in little glades in the woods, where it's moist and cool. It grows off the trails, as though it were a shy deer that could be startled away by noise or quick movements. For these sacred beings, these plants, all problems, in whatever chaotic state they may be, are solved and complete. I roll up their slightly wilted leaves into a long wad, like a large salad rolled into a cigar, and chew through their bitterness, don't stop until I've eaten them all, repeatedly stating my intentions in a kind of murmuring prayer: I ask for help, a gift, or a favour, to see what will happen, what has happened.

While the plant uploads a fractal model of space-time into my mind, I try to write it all down as I remember it. I write, over and over again, for months or even years: about how the unearthly object appeared suddenly, in the middle of the human mind, like a portal to a higher world, a newer world, completely different from what anyone had seen before. Most couldn't perceive, couldn't observe, couldn't even describe the vision, the amazing miracle, the brilliant mosaic, the annihilating orgasm, the unanticipated dimension, the magical wonder, the hidden symbol that appeared in front of Their eyes at that moment, and then at every moment, whatever They were doing. Some reached ecstasy in the bathtub, others on the front lawn, at dinner, while reading, or even while sleeping, within Their dreams, the prophet of the fourth dimension projected into the world of Their senses. They looked at it, these humans of the future who were without the superior brain of the future, even though it was not possible to see. And having seen something the mind couldn't comprehend, They entered the world of four dimensions.

It's difficult to describe what it looked like when the eyelid of my own forehead lifted from my brain's eye; in any case, only part of my brain was allowed to see the transcendental object at the end of time. This cross-dimensional access point to the impossible fourth-person perspective was outside language, and by being outside language it can't be described by language. To describe it through the use of language would be to kill it with language because it's an entity that resists description in language, meaning it's an entity that's the opposite of the hopeful objects created by language. It's an antilanguage.

Regaining control of my brain after reaching the fourth dimension was only a relatively insignificant beginning. Geometric irrelevancies communicated, intermittently. It didn't impress me very much. In fact, the entrancingly language-proof, hyper-dimensional object bored me and made me uncomfortable. The verminous visitor who came to the Earth for me from the fourth dimension, an archangel from an ethereal lair of stellar dust, cast shadows onto our world in the form of Gods. Of course, humans faced only the first one of these Gods, but it was the most insignificant God in an endless line, in an infinite progression of superior Gods, in which each God was twice the God as the one before. An eternal matryoshka doll of gatekeeping Gods. In the womb of every pregnant woman is a pregnant woman who carries in her womb a pregnant woman, until the end of the end, where everything stops.

I know what awaits me in the future: a cloud of black wings hanging above the desert. Flocks of crosses from different planets or different dimensions will take plants and animals away, sucking them into the sky bound and crucified like specimens or artifacts. In fact, I'm waiting for some frightening event, for an explosion to destroy this building, for my heart to stop, or for the end of the world to come—anything just so long as I won't have to go on this way. Maybe afterwards, something will come to Earth to wake the dead. Maybe afterwards, paradise will finally come to Earth.

I'm slowly taken into scenes of the dead returning to life, scenes of changelings clambering, climbing and crawling over ruins. Winged creatures, as pale as insectoid aliens, swarm everywhere. With unnatural eyes, frighteningly sad and without being, They are ineffably indifferent to all that exists. Gods, my God. I can't understand how, but someday, I'll end up like Them.

They're outlined in rainbows and energies with rotating auras that remind me of peacocks, breathing in an overwhelming light with something divine about it, Their postmortal faces shining like biological idiot suns in the burning kingdom of the now.

I used to take comfort in the fact that the world was ending. That every earthly object would soon cease. I feel, as I have during so many nights of fear and cold sweats, the terror of the end of being, the infinity of the nonbeing to come, the disappearance of the world. I can already see my inevitable end: I'll dissolve, make myself a flame of mad ecstasy, flourishing irresistibly as I monstrously unfold on the other shore, the shore where everything flickers and crackles, where I'll spread the rotting light of extinction and erasure like an eternal black fire that never goes out and come to consist of the final present.

I'll let my manuscript burn, too, along with my body and mind. Ash will be the final fate of my writing. All my writing is destined for fire and forgetting. Fire and forgetting will be my only reader. I'm writing only a few final pages now, so my world will not be left unfinished. And these, too, will soon be read, passionately or indifferently, after my death by the same providential fire.

Then I'll have peace.

It's so easy to imagine a world that differs in one or two details from any other, an almost identical world, only in this parallel world, the death of the species doesn't bring about the death of all things. Neither does the end of the human species bring about the end of nature. The end of the Earth itself. The permanence of humans: unnecessary to the permanence of everything else. An unimportant mammal who lived for a brief moment on this Earth's dancing corpse. In fact, since They disappeared, the world's never been so alive. Their very existence feels foreign to this world. Things began before Them, things will not end after Them. There's no end of the world.

My mind collages theories desperately, running on as though it's the only thing awake in the universe. If I stop thinking, my mind becomes clear. It becomes clear that I'm in pain. I don't know if I can even call it pain. It's something that I don't really grasp or see but that is there, like a dagger in the midst of my mind. What I feel, what I experience exceeds ideas of pain altogether. It's as if I'm feeling someone else's pain, every brutal moment, in the flesh of my body, without any connection to me. The pain is like ice shattering. I fall into the freezing water and suddenly I'm underneath, searching for a hole where I can breathe again. But I don't scream in the end, swimming in the limitless, black, frozen water, although I have never felt anything like it, although what I feel scares me.

Sometimes I imagine I'm the groundskeeper of a huge, empty parkland where no one ever comes, and I'm watching over it for no one but myself. History carries on with just one person. The entire inheritance of civilization is for one person. Me, no one but me. Deciding unknowable justice. I can take anything. I can call myself anything. I can proclaim peace anywhere on Earth. At times, I feel less like a consciousness in this world than I do the world itself focusing on a specific scene in the universe of me. And because I represent the only possible continuity of what there was before, I must be the entire world. For the world is nothing but my world. Because the object of my thoughts is my thoughts, and the world is the same as my thoughts.

I'm the last person on Earth.

I feel I have no limits, that everything is possible, that I have not only the algorithm of being but the formula of divinity. Because the world I'm in is generated, moment by moment, just for me. And my consciousness is the projection of a much vaster mind, one I contemplate without being able to understand it. But my mind can't accept, once it imagines totality and eternity, the fact that it's not eternal. I can't accept the fact that to contemplate a universe I know to be incomprehensible, I've been given the mind of a human, a mammalian envelope for this guerilla cognition.

I'm having a paranoid psychedelic experience.

My body ignores me. It moves on its own, separately, in a form deeper than sleep, unburdened by my conscious mind. I can't believe this is my real body, or even a form of my real body. Because I'm not my own body. I have one, but I'm its prisoner. I'm a prisoner of my mind, which is a prisoner of my body, which is a prisoner of the world. Perhaps that's why I speak about myself as if I'm a thing. "It." I don't have a body, but "It" does, the "It" where I live. I wait in "It," in this antechamber of the infinite, locked forever inside the body of a compartmentalized animal, a room enclosed in the most enormous construction I've ever seen, a building whose combination of ancient temple and industrial space horrifies me. It has infinitely thick walls and organic doors to mental agony. Within It, there is nothing to do but die.

So far, the door is still closed. The door on the wall never opens. Through this door, I can get out. But I won't go before I'm supposed to. In the next moment, after extinction, I can grasp the knob firmly, I can turn it, and I can pull it toward me. Opening the door, I can break through the wall and leave the room, with all the risk of leaving.

I sometimes feel I'm in a world without time. That I've always been here, and that I'll always be this way, somewhere in the night before my birth and the day after my death. I walk for endless hours, miserable eternal hours, without anything in my mind, through the continually crossing streets of neighbourhoods that look like evacuated villages. There are houses scattered throughout and on the overlooking forested mountainsides.

There are no signs of humanity here, and the shadows in the sinister darkness of the infrastructure denature everything. Empty and silent houses press against either side of the road—dead houses, all in varying states of decay. One building has collapsed, only the pillars have survived, while others look ready to be lived in.

I spend some time wandering from one house to the next. I can go into any of these ancient houses, into any of Their old rooms, dimly illuminated, these houses with pianos or cellos, with cold hallways, with pots of dusty houseplants withered in the shadows. It seems the inhabitants abandoned these houses in a terrible panic, as if in escape from a devastating natural disaster. They've taken nothing with Them, were seemingly happy to escape with Their own lives. But no one, absolutely no one escaped. Not one other person survived. Absolutely everyone's dead.

I let Them die. I let Them all die.

What's most shocking and frightening about the disappearance of These people is the emptiness of Their rooms. The inhumanity of human constructions, empty of the inhabitants who gave them any use or purpose. I still sense Them here, and I hate it. Where They Themselves should be, there is nothing but these empty rooms. In the kitchen are the dishes They ate from, in the bathrooms are the toothbrushes They used, and in the bedrooms are the beds in which They slept.

Whenever I try to think about Them, I can't seem to find the right words, which makes it impossible for me to think about anything, and that puts me into a terribly confused state—confused and frightened by great and nameless emotions and fighting off images of the sad insanity of my old life, an unresolved picture collapsing at the edges.

I've always been afraid of humans. I'm an anthrophobe. This is why I left the human world behind and walked into the forest. To leave society. Toward a greater desolation, further from others and myself and closer to the shared source of everything. I was nearly in my thirty-third January, approaching the beginning of my Jesus year. Crossing the snow-lined mountains toward the sunny neutrality of an unknown home. Toward the sorrow of literary suicide. I didn't want to turn thirty-three. A point of passage, thirty-three. The passage from a vague foreboding to a senescent scream full of horror, when maturity begins to decline toward old age. I wanted to be dead or immortalized while I was still thirty-two.

I agreed to live. It was all I could do.

Incrementally, as a gradual and evolving process, I left the life I wanted to leave. I used psychedelics, books, writing, my mind, and my body to continue to seek deep and mysterious solitudes and live in that vast, uncontaminated nature of caves and grottoes in the mountains, to regain the lost wisdom of wolves, where there would never be anybody. I felt, surprisingly and gratefully, empowered. But just as a human's body has limbs and joints and organs, so does my body. And as an ex-human with a human's body, I'm also the last human, my last enemy, and so the only way this fear can disappear is if I do.

I'm afraid of myself now—much more afraid than I've ever been before. I fear my face the way I've never feared anything else in the world. I've never feared anything in my life with such intensity. I don't know what I would've been like if the world hadn't ended. I was almost human then. But I'm all through as a human being now. The human is leaving my bloodstream, as if it had never existed. All I am is the lingering memory of what They used to be. I live and will die among ruins, in the saddest circumstances on the face of the Earth.

I write in the dark, without any breaks, repeating this story to myself, each version highlighting a new aspect of my experience, and analyzing it accordingly, in the psychic trajectory of white pages in this title-less text by an anonymous author, the autobiography of an unknown person as enigmatic as a faceless god. No story has any meaning if it's not a revelation, if it doesn't have the delicate brutality of revelation, like a gospel in which everything becomes unimaginably complicated, hopeless, and absurd. But I want this story to be more like a church, simply made but expressive, and I'd like God to be living in this story, as in a church.

I'm not writing so that someone will read my words. I'm writing to try to understand what's happening to me. And I'll reiterate here, for eternity, again and again, this story of endless, hopeless torture, the most terrifying story of all the infernal paradises and celestial hells: one that gives the greatest sense of the world after the end of the world. Not only the sense that the world is the end of everything that there is in the world, but that the only thing there is in the world is the end of the world. The unimaginable end of existence.

I try to disengage from my thoughts and just listen to the total silence of the ruined chapel. The room is soft. There's a spiderweb in the corner of the ceiling covered with dangling insect larvae. They're suspended from glistening, translucent threads. I look at the spiderweb complex that seems absurd and extravagant—a mansion with thousands of rooms, each a different size, fitting in every direction.

A spider's mind is not in its brain or in its body. It extends into its web, into the territory it inhabits. The web is the organ with which the spider understands everything that happens in the world. And if part of its web is damaged, the spider acts as if part of its mind is damaged. Humans aren't like this. They shrivelled up in Their webs by the millions. Webs of glittering ghosts. That's what I dislike about Them. They didn't care, the fucks. Whoever They were. The They that's the It that's the Human. They couldn't see the darkness and the spider-face beyond and the great web of it all. Their minds were like impenetrable cerebral fortresses locked away inside Their heads, not a garden where many species live together. This is how They should've been.

I travel in a circle with no beginning or end. I come and go like a busy ant without a colony, changing places, since no matter how much I walk, this way or that way, I'm always where I was before, because one place is as good as any other when you are alone in the circle of a valley without exit. I'll stay, forever, the prisoner of this valley that's as uncrossable as a sea without shores. Because I know now that I can't leave this valley alone, that together we'll rot in the homogeneous pitch black of the earth, an ooze of humankind. I'm bound to my fellow sufferer, all the dead people, in a cathedral of spiders, in an ecology of souls, to all Those who will soon be erased from the world because my world will soon end too, along with my manuscript.

The certainty of dying is given at birth. Life is a disease, sexually transmitted, ending in death. Wherever I am, death will find me. And death takes nothing but what is born. It'll take nothing but what it took from me on the day I was born, and because I was born for the sake of living, I live in fear of death. Because I live, because I was born. Because I was born, I must not believe that my life should continue. And because I came into this world from a frightening abyss without memories, I must suffer unimaginably, and will soon perish, all in an instant, as though I'd never lived, as though I'd never been born.

I'm a doomed person. I have no emotions, no attachments, no property, and no name. Everything in me is wholly absorbed in a single thought and a single passion. In the very depths of my being, I know that I have broken all bonds that tie me to the human world. Between that world and me there exists only a relentless and irreconcilable war to the death. A science of destruction, a science without an object. But I expect no mercy. And I must accustom myself to torture. Because for me, there exists only one thought, one aim: the success of extinction. The cold and single-minded passion for death.

It's better to not be than to be.

Death's a much better salvation than creation. It vests a power of impersonal negation, a Not I. Only in death do we find true happiness, a happiness that resides in complete tranquility and peace and that comes only with death, the utter nothingness of annihilation. Striving toward this end, I now prepare to destroy myself and to destroy with my own hands everything that stands in the path of extinction.

The future is no longer my problem. One of my problems is my inability to recognize and accept my own extinction. Not to correct my extinction but to accustom myself to it. I don't know about extinction. It may well be that I can never fully adapt to my own extinction. I take extinction to be extinction and, having taken extinction to be extinction, I think of extinction, think of extinction, think of extinction, think, *This is my extinction*, and my extinction seems natural. Because all extinction looks equally extinct to me.

But the insane spiral of extinction is as broad as a maelstrom, becoming more and more hysterical, as the divine transforms into the obscene, geometry into chaos, angels into monsters. I can't stop myself from envisioning the tragic disorder of the faces hidden in the depths of extinction, the twisted innards in the centre, the smiling void that no one else will ever see. I look into Their minds, I read Their thoughts, I feel Their trials, Their silences, Their orgasms, Their moments of illumination. They no longer see through Their own eyes and no longer think with Their own minds. I see and hear everything for Them, as though I were holding, in my palm, Their own heads.

I know I'm decaying, that my mind is a pool of vomit, and still I can do nothing but scream like someone being tortured underground while watching as the fabric of my body, preserved in torment, is eviscerated alive. The torture will never pause and never end, because, as I always realize, as soon as these terrors, terrors greater than anything, wrap me inside the dense horror of their sticky obsidian web, trap my arms, legs, and throat, leaving my body helpless, I'm in hell, in that version of hell made for me and me alone, my own personal hell, here, in this world, where devils pull off all my limbs, limbs that grow back only to be pulled off again and again, limbs that will grow back forever, ready to suffer again and again and again and again, without rest, without time, without space, and without memory. Just pure pain.

There's no return to a time before pain, before me. The anatomy of pain pervades everything.

I walk out of my hermitage, the last outposts of the human world and into the endless tapestry of sound in the green sanctuary of the surrounding forest. The trail through the woods begins here. I take a ferned road that flanks a deep chasm, high above the suicidal blackness of a stream. The eroded scars of ancient wheels have made this long-abandoned road a decaying ruin. When there's no road, I forge a path of my own.

A deer drinks out of the cold stream below. The noise of the stream blocks its ability to survey me. It tries to compensate quickly, with glances, and then it drinks again before moving back into a quieter, more remote place.

I climb to the top of a mountain. Its height calls me. I want to have it, and so I ascend it, for no other reason than to dominate it. High above, I see the wide horizon. But none of it is mine. I can't possess the mountain. What I see isn't within me. I look down over the panorama of fields and roads and rivers and cloud-obliterated cities with some peripheral suburbs bordering woodland and wind farms. There's a wind grazing the ground, dragging flurries of fine snow and soot. Everything has the aura of an indescribable loneliness, the loneliness you might find in the grand churches, unmoving and frighteningly quiet.

The sound that I enjoy most is the sound of the silence on the top of the mountain. I can't hear a bird, a cricket. I can't hear a ripple on a lake. I can't hear the wind going through the pines. But I do have a sense of space here. And then, once I get over the summit of the mountain, the whole topology of the surrounding landscape is revealed to me, and the many layers of its quietude come toward me, and I know exactly where I am.

I paid a lot of attention to people, but I really should've paid a lot more attention to what was all around me. People created a lot of noise. Without people there's much more silence. Not an absence of sound, but an absence of noise. I now have a sense of presence, of where I am and what I am. Of course, wildlife is still busy communicating.

Wherever I go, colour retreats and the world turns black-and-white. I've been wandering these temporal mirages for what seems like many lifetimes, always descending, in an imperceptible advance toward nowhere, while it becomes darker and darker, a desolate dusk erasing everything. The installation of night spreads its spider legs and the entire sky collapses over me. I'm alone in this giant valley of the dead. There is only life and death in flesh, and death's a sort of exit. I open my hands to reveal my lifeline, luckline, and loveline. In the middle of each palm is a capital *M*, which in this underworld could stand only for *Mort*, death.

I descend the mountain and emerge into a large meadow framed by distant lines of shadowy trees and low hills. I sit down in the blank frost of a field of grass at the edge of an orchard to get some rest and a thunderstorm rolls over me, a truly apocalyptic storm. Black snow falls. And while I lie there, the thunder echoes through the valley, and I hear the deep texture of all the insects and frogs and longleaf needles. A terrestrial soundtrack. I simply take it all in. Lying on my back, with my eyes open. Without needing to know what I'm doing here, how I got here, or when I'm going home. I stay here, without destiny, waiting for my life to end in a world without end.

I'm just a ghost, a hauntologist, haunting myself, but I'll soon be free of every trail. Ghost and all.

The sky is the colour of snake venom. Shadows and light flicker across the mountain landscape as the clouds run above, alternately revealing and obscuring the sun. A sun that neither comes up nor sets and that seems to close for me not the last day but a day that comes after all the other days—last in the sense of the time when days were still days, like the last day when humankind understood what a day was.

The listening horizon extends for many miles in every direction. I hear the high-pitched twittering of a winter wren. I hear the bugling of an elk call further away. Guttural, adrenaline filled, male and wild. Even further away is the sound of the river draining the forest into a glacial lake. It echoes off the far side of the valley.

The wind from the lake, from its opposing shore, is penetrating. The end of the end is in view. I shudder but not from the cold and, scanning the dark waters, consider my writing. All of my writing is a huge lake. I'm a mere stream in search of the waters of oblivion. All that matters is feeding the lake. I don't really matter. The lake matters. I must keep feeding the lake with my writing, until it has all my writing.

When I reach the beach, it's musical. Sublime symphonies hidden away in gigantic driftwood logs. Lonely interior fugues. The sand that holds the lake in place is a spell. The lake is not a real lake but some scintillating sea or oneiric ocean. I imagine humanity's fossils, everyone's bones arranged in the sands by the dark waters of this ocean terminus. I've walked so long to get here, to the end of the Earth, back to the sea, to the original waters, in a true regression to the ocean, but however long it may have been, it's not an eternity. I listen and the wood fibres of nature's instruments vibrate, excited by the sound of the ocean.

I watch the water until dark falls and the surface of the water reflects nothing. I float on top of the water, my spine against its surface, my head hanging far back, deeply sunk into the water. Then I plunge into the sea and swim with my gaze always turning back toward the land away from which I continue inexorably to move. I drink in the saltiness. Feel a wave across my body. Immerse in the moisture of the Other. Change happens in waves.

It's painless to let go.

The tide turns eternal as I drown myself in the sea. I swim out, keep swimming, let myself be enfolded in the deep. It flows over me in a cold that isn't physical but like silence: the silence of uncreating. Beyond all the burning waves of purple, nothing but nonbeing shows. I become the sea and its waves. I become everything and I become nothing. I unfold across time like naked clarity of thought in a visible language. My body is my meaning. It runs through everything, and it takes many, many forms, endless forms and endless manifestations—life-forms or even idea-forms, thought-forms. I become my meaning and behold the meaning I become: the unification of inner and outer life. I see things new. There's awe, it's all awe.

I close my eyes and the world is lost.

Continual Gehenna

Nothing is more difficult than to turn oneself into a saint. To kneel in a vault and die beneath a robe of homicidal stone, without light, without horizon, as intangible as a corpse in the grave.

While chanting, the hermit nun sat in a chair garnished with a hundred long nails, and when she felt herself falling into the blooms of oblivion, she pressed her shoulders firmly against the sharp points. There was nothing better for bringing her back to reality and recalling her wandering attention.

In her soul there was a sort of triptych of glowing glass. Sorrow filled the centre panel, while, on either side, was one of fear, the other of unfulfilled hope. The windows overlooked a transparent field of dead moons. Sometimes forlorn figures seemed to rise from the earth to scorn their conditions. Sometimes they floated over the appalling depths or descended on solitary peaks in the hideous mineral landscape where there was no sign of life or movement, only endless mountains hiding the tabernacle of clouds. With no hope of escaping from the Gehenna of the flesh, these liminal beings had turned away with disappointment from the sky, which had lost all its wholeness, all its immeasurability in that ominous place of perpetual dread. For the mountains not only made the sky look small and passionless in the blaze of daylight, but also attracted the chimerical creatures with hairy human faces and enormous colourless eyes full of etherealized heaven to the ravines below—whose horrible immensity was in the wrong place, stolen from above and cast into the vast spiraling pits of blackness, into the very engines of everlasting hell.

They held the symbolic instruments of their death, like soldiers bearing arms, a dismal procession of four-footed bodies with horned heads and outstretched wings feathered with scales forever tempted by labyrinths, moving one by one, one after another, single file on the narrow path that edged the motionless swell of the mountaintops. And by degrees this long line of silent shades spied the cruciform mold of the tombs that the angels had erected, where the bodies of the saints were reposing, sheltered behind the sacred bulwarks of a cloister, hidden at the bottom of the valley.

The holy silence became painful. It was a relief when the nails pierced the nun's skin to remind her to recite the prayers, verse after verse. Like dripping tears, she repeated the rippling melody at regular intervals, slowly and religiously. But her features were now as unknown as her passions. Around her head was an extraordinary nimbus of sinister eloquence, a halo composed of a peacock's tail with gilt porcupine quills.

Through the screen of amorphous nothing, standing out like a celestial vision in the spiderweb of the nun's soul, the outline of the steeple's seraphic dissemblance emerged, toward which the liminal animals pushed their way. Its vertical word stood out against the anonymous menace of terrain, as if hovering there in the elemental forces that rose up around it. It belonged to the planet, to the meaningless passivity of the inert. To raw, mute reality itself.

With a handful of earth, the phantoms entered the narthex of purgatory. Everything under the forest roof of the mythical cathedral had become lost in a furnace of purple. Water stilled with mystification, swallowing the shadows of the things it reflected. In its basin of sorrow was a continued and profound absorption of forgotten sensation. Noiselessly, they passed through the successive phases of the nave and the aisles, crossing the transept and the choir. Until, surrounded by a crown of chapels, they had at last reached the top of the tree of the living cross. Where, in the ataraxy of the apse, with its monstrance altar of golden molten fire and its suffering statuary solemnly representing the mediatrix of pardon in melancholy decay, obscure mutilations stripped away the secret holy fear of impersonal fecundity from the faceless generous mother.

The spectacle of the sanctuary's silent world bewitched these terrestrial shades, who had become playthings for its deep portal of eschatological visions and evil augury. Incapable of stopping themselves from entering a diabolical manoeuvre of vertiginous descent toward an ever more profound void of sacramental darkness, the humanity animal traced one of their figures of geomancy in blasphemous blood. In the barbaric grace of heathen prayer, they whirled around like a massacre of monks in a sacrilegious dance, their eyeballs in ecstasy, their mouths gaping with perfidious laughter, some screaming aloud in lament. Others, in still more pagan moods of absurd dogma, squatted with arms raised and heads shaking, as if by doing so they could make the world not be. And the earth trembled and opened up and exposed the great door with a tympanum in a pointed arch bearing the presentation of the apocalypse, a gate to the origin of the unknown, which was itself another secret: a key that opened nothing.

www.ingramcontent.com/pod-product-compliance
Lightning Source LLC
Chambersburg PA
CBHW070423310726
48977CB00003B/805